the RELIC

...the eternal search

the RELIC

Ashwin Karthik
&
Madhava Sharma

Published in 2018 by www.pblishing.com

Marketed by

Maple Press Private Limited
Sales Office A 63, Sector 58, Noida 201 301, U.P., India
phone +91 120 455 3581, 455 3583
email info@**maple**press.co.in
website www.**maple**press.co.in

ISBN: 978-93-87348-06-6

10 9 8 7 6 5 4 3 2 1

Contents

Synopsis

"Vijay stuck his ear on the door and pressed the eye of the cobra as if he pressed a button, he heard a latch unfasten itself. Immediately the two halves of the door started to slide in their respective sides. With a creaking noise, the legendary door slid open."

The story of "The Relic" revolves around the Sree Padmanabha Swamy Temple in Kerala – the treasure it holds and the mystery around it. The tale begins with the government trying to find out whether the money had been misappropriated.

Vijay an Intelligence Bureau officer, is sent with orders to open the secret vaults of the Sree Padmanabha Swamy temple. He finds ways to open the vault and is particularly fascinated by a pot he finds in a metal box, amid heaps of the golden ornaments and precious gems.

After completing the formal investigations, he sets out to find out for himself the secret behind the pot.

The Relic is a journey of the officer on his quest to unravel the mystery behind the pot and incorporated into the plot is the intrigue of the Aghoris in Banaras – some of them practice rituals that are gory and grisly.

It talks of ascetics and their divine yogic powers, through which they could teleport their souls into other people's bodies. It also talks about astrology and also warns how people in the modern world are being misled by the fake astrologers.

The story is both a thriller and an insightful glimpse into the protagonist's mind, that incorporates Vijay's personal life and his curious past.

Acknowledgment

First of all we thank the Almighty for inspiring us to write the story and enabling us to complete it. We thank our families and friends especially our mothers for the people we are.

We are grateful to Mr. Subramani L. for suggesting the title for our book "The Relic". We also thank Mrs. Mavis Mendonca Smith and Mrs. Rathnaprabha for the primary editing of the book. Last but not the least we thank all the co-funders without whose support this book wouldn't have become a reality.

CHAPTER 1

It was 1 a.m. at night. Vijay, a celebrated officer in the Intelligence Bureau of India, jolted back to reality from a strange dream. Certainly, he had dreamt about something very disturbing. To try to go back to sleep for another couple of hours would be futile. Sleeplessness only allowed him to toss in his bed restlessly.

Vijay got up from his bed and looked at his watch. It read 18 March, 3 a.m. Vijay had a hunch that the real reason behind his restlessness was his stepfather's medical condition. His stepfather was his pillar of strength; his guardian angel, the man who had adopted him and had given him an opportunity to lead a dignified life,retired officer Major Vikramaditya who, for a decade, was suffering from the fatal disease called multiple sclerosis.

His gut feeling told him something was terribly wrong. So, he decided to take the first morning flight to Bangalore and see his father in the army hospital.

Multiple sclerosis is a demyelinating disease in which the protective coverings of the nerve fibres in the brain and the spinal cord are damaged. This damage disrupts the ability of the nervous system to communicate smoothly with the rest of the body, resulting in a range of signs and symptoms. The symptoms generally include physical, mental and psychiatric problems. Specific symptoms can include double vision, blindness in one eye, weakness of muscles, lack of sensation, or trouble with coordination.

The disease has several forms-with new symptoms either occurring in isolated attacks (relapsing forms) or building up over time (progressive forms). Between two consecutive attacks, symptoms may disappear completely. However, permanent neurological problems often remain, especially as the disease advances.

Loneliness and struggle that Vijay had to endure throughout his childhood never let him get over the death of his biological grandfather. However, Major Vikramaditya had given a new lease of life. There wasn't a day when Vijay didn't feel grateful to him. There wasn't a moment when he had forgotten him and remember him. Vijay's mental trauma had increased ever since the health of the Major deteriorated. The thought of the physical and mental trauma that the Major was going through troubled Vijay constantly.

Vijay had completely drowned himself in work in order to escape from the guilt of not being able to help his father figure.

To distract his restless mind, he began his daily fitness routine of a three-mile jog, significant count of push-ups, multiple sets of three-minute plank exercises and endless number of crunches. After such workout session, no one can think of anything but rest. But still Vijay was not able to put the thought of the Major out of his mind.

He had a mind that was trained to stay focused under situations of extreme pressure. He had to stare death in the eye multiple times in his career, as he was one of the master spies India had produced. His calm demeanour and his ability to think radically under pressure had earned him the title of 'The spy who had come in from the cold.' Still, deep down in his heart, he never could get over the Major's illness.

The only thing he wished for was his father was good health and it was the only thing that could bring him peace. He remained troubled, as he was unable to help the Major. Unable to see his son suffer silently Major Vikramaditya, a couple of years ago, had decided to stay on his own in an old age home supported by the Indian army, so that Vijay couldn't see him suffer.

Couple of months ago, as major Vikramaditya's health had deteriorated, he was admitted to the army hospital. He had entirely lost coordination and sensitivity in his body.

Under the shower, Vijay's mind played the echo of his father's unbearable cry of pain and desperation.

The shrill ringtone of his mobile brought Vijay back to reality. He saw the word 'Bureau' blinking on his mobile screen. Vijay picked up the call and heard a deep voice on the other end of the call ordering him to reach the Bureau in the next 30 minutes.

Vijay told himself that first he would go to the Bureau and find out why he was summoned—then he would take permission to travel to Bangalore.

Thirty minutes later, Vijay was sitting in the air-conditioned cabin of the head of the Intelligence Bureau, in the office of the Ministry of Home Affairs of India, Delhi. He was being asked to pack his bag and travel to Trivandrum to finish what he had begun five years ago.

He was being sent to Trivandrum to investigate the truth behind the doors of the secret vaults in the Sree Anantha Padmanabha Swamy Temple, where the royal family had been accused of mismanagement and misappropriation of temple assets. Four of the doors were regularly opened. The remaining two, denoted A and B by the court were said to be locked for centuries.

The Supreme Court because of public sentiments interrupted the investigation. Led by the new Cabinet, the

Supreme Court had ordered the authorities to resume the probe into the last unopened vault of the temple, which is believed to be guarded by a giant serpent.

He also was informed that he was commanded to leave for Trivandrum immediately and there was no room for delay.

A tussle began between the son Vijay, and the IB officer Vijay—the son urged him to go and see his sick father and the officer in him reminded of his duty. He was in a fix; confused about what call to take. Finally, he decided to call up his father, talk to him, and comfort and assure his father that he would go and see him as soon as he would finish his assignment at Trivandrum.

Later that evening, at home, when Vijay sat alone in his couch, his mind carried him back to the last days of the year of 2010—to his last and the most high-profile investigation with India's ATS (Anti-Terrorist Squad). It was the terror attack at the Taj Hotel of Mumbai, infamously known as the 26/11 attack.

There, he did play a major role in tracking down Abu Rashid, one of the masterminds behind the Mumbai attack. Vijay went to Pakistan as an undercover agent. He was responsible for tracking down Abu's immediate family.

The Intelligence Bureau and the ATS planned to prove to the Saudi Arabian government that the suspect was indeed the mastermind behind the terror attack that shook the world,by matching the DNA of his son Imran with Abu himself.

It was primarily Vijay's idea to track Abu's family, to play the role of a *mochi* (cobbler) and get the blood sample of Imran. Vijay did this by pricking a tiny nail of his foot while mending his shoe. For this accomplishment of his out of many,his efforts were recognized and he was awarded with the Kirti Chakra. Vijay was one of very few cops to be awarded the Kirti Chakra, as it is generally reserved for the armed forces.

After returning from Pakistan in May 2011, he was promoted to the IB, where he was included in the expert committee that was formed by the Supreme Court of India.

Vijay was not happy on being pulled out of action from the field and being ordered to go and solve a petty case of mismanagement of funds in a temple. However, he had to eventually agree based on the reasons for choosing him as a part of the expert committee.

The top reason being his accomplishments as a master spy. Seizing of Abu Rashid by the National Security Agencies spoke volumes of Vijay's capabilities and contribution to national security. His strategies and communication skills were strong enough to make many anti-nationalists spill the beans about the conspiracies and attacks.

Hence, the top officials believed that his skills would prove more than useful in getting vital information from the royal family, temple priests, authorities or the locals of Trivandrum. Given the background Vijay had with security, his presence would certainly help.

The second reason for choosing him was for the easy access he would have into the temple. Vijay being a Namboodiri Brahmin, would not or would rarely be questioned by the temple authorities. His ability to communicate in the local language would come in handy in convincing people to share whatever they know about the investigation.

The third reason for choosing Vijay being the fact that the person who recommended Vijay in the committee knew that he didn't believe in things he didn't see. This would help the committee in being unbiased in matters related to religion.

The last reason, but most important reason,for choosing him was to oversee the security arrangements in Trivandrum as the security agencies and the top court of the country expected turbulence in the city and the state when the secret vaults would to be unlocked.

It was a secret the world was after, but Vijay wasn't keen to go back to that city, which parted him from his roots especially his grandfather. As fate had it for him, Vijay was on the next plane to Trivandrum. Like every day, he called up Major Vikramaditya to enquire about his health and informed him about his next mission.

Trivandrum was buzzing with the rumours that the expert committee was about to damage the shrine, which was believed to hide limitless wealth in its womb. The locals, led by the city's so-called groups of culture protection and a few rowdy politicians had gathered, at the airport.

They were shouting slogans, carrying placards and had tied black ribbons around their arms. They even burnt effigies of the committee members. The protest against the expert committee setting foot on the soil of Trivandrum did not inhibit the committee members.

The local police had to use tear gas and air shots to make sure the officials reached the government guest house safe, as the protesters didn't shy away from setting the government vehicles and parts of the airport reception ablaze.

When the committee members and the government officials tried to convince the residents of the city that they were there only to explore the truth of the temple and not to tamper with their culture and heritage, the people of Trivandrum simply did not want the committee to enter the city.

It was evident even from the behaviour of the local police officials, who passed comment through gritted teeth that even they weren't convinced with the Supreme Court's decision to enter the adobe of the almighty with an intent of exploring the secrets, which the Supreme Power wants to hide from mankind.

With great care, the local police led by M. K. Nair, the Superintendent of Kerala police, Trivandrum, made sure that the team of experts reached the government guest house safe. That evening, the Superintendent again came to the guest house to meet the committee, especially Vijay. He said,

"Sir, as you saw in the morning, the situation in the city is pretty tense. Hence, with due government approvals, I have arranged tight security across the city—especially near the temple and other sensitive areas of the city. Starting today, till the temple raid is successfully completed, the security personnel equipped with weapons will be posted in disguise of the locals.

"If you think anything else is required regarding security, let me know and I will get it arranged."

Vijay appreciated the officer's concern and told him that he personally would go and have a look at the arrangements and then would get back with suggestions.

Vijay decided to take a walk around the city, well-disguised with an artificial beard and a moustache.

He even got dressed in the local attire (dhoti and shirt),so that people would not know who he really was.

Pretending to be a tourist in the city who did not know the way to the Padmanabha Swamy Temple, he hired a rickshaw to drive him to the temple. On the way, Vijay started a conversation with him. After some sweet talk, he brought out the topic of the Supreme Court sending an expert committee to explore if there indeed was any hidden treasure in the temple as it was claimed.

The driver stopped short in the busy road, angrily slapped his head and let out a stream of Malayalam curses against those questioning the honesty of the royal family. Vijay got a taste of the emotions the locals had about the royal family and the divinity of the temple and their opinion on who should take control of the wealth of the temple, if it is unearthed.

Vijay reached the Sree Anantha Padmanabha Swamy Temple Street. It was a place vivid in his memory! It was the place where he used to live 15 years ago. A vivid image surfaced of a 12-year-old holding his dead grandfather's head on his lap, who also happened to be the chief priest of the Sree Anantha Padmanabha Swamy temple. He was suffocated to death and his house had caught fire, for reasons unknown.

This happened when Vijay was away playing with friends. A couple of boys finally were able to find him, after looking for him in most places where he could play. When he returned, the fire was burning in its full might. The kid looked for his grandfather and when he could not find him, barged into the burning house. He escaped the clasp of the onlookers, who were trying to extinguish the fire, and he entered the house. Seeing the kid trying to save his grandfather, a few mustered up their courage to help him.

But it was too late. By the time the old man was dragged out he only had enough time to caress his grandson's cheek. He tried telling something to the boy but failed. Vijay was devastated after the incident, as the old man was the only family he had, after his parents had died in a train crash. Losing the only family he had, Vijay felt numb. He couldn't shed even a drop of tear.

After performing the last rites of his grandfather with the guidance of some temple priests, Vijay had nowhere to go. He felt as if he was falling into an endless crevasse. After spending couple of days in the ruined house, beneath the oil painting of the Lord that hung on the wall, he realized that he had to carve his own path in life.

Vijay's grandfather always wanted him to be a self-made man. Hence not expecting anyone to come to his aid, Vijay stepped into the dark to an unknown future. He tried to fetch a way of earning for himself but failed. One day, when he was seeking work that could feed him, he fell unconscious. He was without a drop of water or a morsel of food for days. He had developed weakness and fever because of starvation.

An ex-army officer, Vikramaditya, who had lost one of his limbs, was visiting Trivandrum to seek peace at the Lord's feet, spotted Vijay in one of the platform of the bus station of the city. He brought him to Bangalore, where he resided alone and cared for him. Vikramaditya had lost his family in a train crash when they were travelling to see him in Gujarat army hospital, where he was being treated.

For the injuries he had during the mission, he had successfully accomplished to ignore his own safety.

As Vikramaditya wasn't being able to accept the bitter reality that he had to lead the rest of life alone, he was shattered from within. The wounds and pain that he had sustained in the battlefield and during the various mission couldn't tamper his will to survive, his grit to live. Even the loss of his limb hadn't defeated his enthusiasm and spirit towards life. However, the loss of his family did.

After being forced to retire from the armed forces, due to the loss of a limb and the loss of his kith and kin, Major Vikramaditya felt he had nothing to live for. He had to quit the army, which served the greatest motivation in his life and he had no one to call his own.

Fortunately, he felt that it was Lord Padmanabha's wish that he noticed Vijay in the bus station and felt compassionate about the young boy. Vikramaditya decided to take him along with himself and care for him. Taking care for Vijay made Major

Vikramaditya feel as if he was caring for his own son. He would stay awake all night and take care of the boy, unless the doctor assured that Vijay was fine.

The Major soon began to nurture the dream to grow Vijay as his son. After a couple of weeks, when Vijay was stable and wanted to take a leave, he was asked about his whereabouts. It was at that moment, when Vijay narrated his past. He was asked to stay along and study in the army school but given Vijay's self-esteem, he hesitated. Vikramaditya then offered to educate and be his guardian in return of the domestic help he could offer. Vijay agreed. In due course, they shared a father-son relationship and ultimately, Vikramaditya officially adopted Vijay.

But it was the memory of his past that had not let Vijay return to Trivandrum for such a long time. But deep within he was never detached from neither the city nor his past. Now after ages he was standing on the street in which, one of the houses was where he was born. But he felt as a stranger in his own city.

Vijay went to an old house, which stood charred. What remained of its door fell apart, when he pushed it open. Spiders had made the walls their own, with cobwebs all over. The entrance had no door as it was burnt and broken. Vijay was guessing it could be the house, where he learnt to walk holding his grandfather's fingers.

The moment the saw a huge oil painting of Lord Vishnu in eternal yogic sleep, laced with many generations of cobwebs, he was sure that this was indeed his house. Vijay's eyes became moist on remembering himself running around the house as a kid,giving a tough time to his grandfather looking for him,especially when he stayed out late at night, roaming in some street and his grandfather had to come looking for him.

It was ironical that just beneath the painting of the Lord was lying a drunkard, unconscious because of huge amount of alcohol consumption, along with generations of spiders, cockroaches and other insects crawling around.

Vijay found it bitter to remember how his house was brightly lit with lamps at dusk till dawn—how the air used to be filled with the rich fragrance of incense sticks. But now, his house had not seen brightness for ages and was filled with the rotten smell of rodent droppings.

Though Vijay seemed to be a cold and ruthless intelligence officer from the outside, he was an emotional and caring person from within. How he wished he could have grown up in the love and care of his parents and the pampering of his grandfather! But all he was left with was a few memories and an old house, which could crumble anytime and be one with the very dust that covered it.

He could never forgive himself for not being there when his grandfather needed him the most.

Chapter 2

After the brief nostalgic break, Vijay was back to his ruthless best. He knew he had to get cracking on the job he had been sent for. He decided to learn what the residents of the city feel about the royal family being accused of mismanagement of the temple funds. The first thing he did was to spot a store, which sold sacred things.

He picked up a poonal (sacred thread used to perform upanayanam; an elaborate ritual of confirming a Namboodiri boy as a Brahman and for initiating him to Brahmachaari.) He knew that the thread was capable of getting him an access to any part of the temple. Though personally he is an atheist and never wanted to enter a temple, in order to do his duty he had to make an exception.

After donning the poonal, Vijay went towards the temple's east-facing main entrance. The nataka sala is on this side of the temple. The nataka sala is where, Kathakali, a famous traditional dance form in Kerala, is performed as part of a 10-day festival held every year during the months of Meenamand Thulam. Meenam corresponded to the English months of March-April, and Thulam corresponded to the English months of October-November.

There he saw people entering the temple without wearing their shirt along the pathway from the pond, Padmatheertham, after washing their feet in the holy water.

Vijay entered the corridor of the temple. This corridor was filled with hundreds of granite pillars steeped in beautiful elaborate carvings. These intricately sculpted pillars stand as testimony to the fabulous architectural marvels of the entire temple.

As he walked around looking for someone whom he could talk to, he spotted an old man, dressed in a dhoti, with a wispy, white beard that trailed down to his waist, and a pitchfork-shaped tilaka smeared on his forehead. The tilaka is drawn everyday on the forehead, usually after the daily bath, signifies enlightenment. This man suddenly had a severe asthma attack, while reading out and explaining the verses from the Bhagvat Gita to the gathering in the temple. Vijay rushed to the aid of the old man. He helped the old man find his inhaler and regain his composure.

When he tried to resume reading the holy book, Vijay requested him to take rest and offered to do the reading himself. He continued reading from where the former had left.

Karmanye vadhikaraste Ma Phaleshu Kadachana,

Ma Karmaphalaheturbhurma Te Sangostvakarmani

"You have the right only to work but never to expect its fruits. Let not the fruits of action be your motive, nor let your attachment be to inaction."

Vijay continued with his explanation of the verses. He said, "We only have the power and the right to do our work. We are not empowered to either choose or anticipate the fruits of our work, which is in the hands of God above. Hence, it is prudent to live without any worldly motives. When a man trains himself to live like this and this habit becomes ingrained within him, he will soon realize that working without seeking the fruits of labour is a great way to live."

Vijay's explanation continued, "Do good work without any kind of desire to be free. Even if you choose to do good to achieve heaven, this desire is selfish as it binds you down instead of allowing you to be free."

While closing the book after completed the brief explanation of the verse, Vijay remembered his training in the NSG as a youngster. That training is what helped him play a priest's role perfectly during the investigation of the terror attack at the Akshardham Temple in Gujarat.

Staying in the Akshardham premises, Vijay played a major role in collecting various sets of articles, which were used by the forensics to analyze the samples and track the origin of the conspiracy.

The offer made to read the Gita was a masterstroke, as it allowed Vijay to strike a cordial relation with the old man. The old man thanked Vijay a great deal for helping him regain his composure. When asked who he was, Vijay used the same trick of introducing himself as an NRI from the Middle East. He was here to salute the temple deity, with his dead grandfather's ashes and then scatter it on Indian soil, which was the old man's dying wish. Vijay also mentioned that he wished to perform his grandfather's death ceremony and other rituals here in Trivandrum, so that his soul rest in peace.

As the old man was immensely impressed with Vijay's authority over the Bhagvat Gita, he asked Vijay how he had mastered the Gita at such a young age.

Vijay explained that it was his grandfather from whom he inherited the fondness and inclination towards the reading of the Gita and other spiritual scriptures. He used to accompany his father to the same temple in his childhood to read the Holy Scriptures. He used to read the Gita every evening at home even in the Middle East. "Maybe, that was the reason he wanted to breath his last in the abode of the Supreme Lord. It was my negligence that I did not fulfill his wish in time." Vijay shed tears in remembrance of his grandfather.

In return, the old man introduced himself as Raghuraman, a historian by profession and a story teller by choice. He chose to visit the temple every day, as he could not find better stories than about the lord himself.

Mr. Raman appreciated the affection Vijay had for his grandfather. He consoled him by telling him that his grandfather's soul will feel happy seeing his grandson was doing so much for him even after his death.

After catching his breath and relaxing for a while, Mr. Raman got up to go home. Vijay asked the old man to wait for a while, as he would walk him home after a quick salutation to the lord. Though helping Mr. Raman was important, Vijay was also interested because the old man was an historian and could give him vital information about the history of the temple.

On the way to Mr. Raman's house, it was the old man who began the conversation. He asked Vijay whether it his first visit to India. Vijay answered "no" and said that he had come to India multiple times on business. But yes, it was his first personal visit. Moreover, it was his first time to Trivandrum. Unfortunately, his first visit to the hometown of his ancestors had to be with the ashes of his beloved grandfather.

To change the mood of the conversation, Mr. Raman asked Vijay about his experience in the temple. Vijay said it was the most serene and divine experience he had ever had in his life. Now he knew why his grandfather wanted him to bow down at this abode of the Lord.

He added that this temple was very different from most other temples he had visited in various parts of the country. Vijay said he was quite enamoured and overwhelmed with the beauty and size of the Sree Anantha Padmanabha Swamy Temple with its splendid seven storeyed gopuram constructed over the eastern entrance, the towering flagpole that can be seen when one enter through the eastern entrance, the nine intricately carved entrances, and large number of water sources found all over the temple.

Mr. Raman was amazed at the attention to detail that Vijay mentioned in his explanation of the temple. Mr. Raman did initially think that Vijay appeared overtly inquisitive when he went on to ask whether his observations about the temple were right and if so, what made these characteristics of temple unique. But the retired but passionate historian in him was way too excited to respond to Vijay's queries on the historic monument to think as to why the young man was so interested in these questions, which are not usually asked by common tourists and pilgrims.

Mr. Raman nodded in agreement and said that Vijay's observations were right. These were the very characters that made this temple stand out from among most others in the country.

He continued, "But before anything I want to tell you the speciality of the main shrine. The main deity of the temple Sree Anantha Padmanabha Swamy is in a reclining position. He lies on divine serpent, Adi Sesha, whose enormous hood seems to protect and cover the Lord's head. The entire idol is made with 12,000 saligramams, black stones considered very sacred by the Hindus and found specifically on the banks of the Gandaki River that runs through the high and majestic Himalayan Mountains of Nepal.

The 80-feet flagpole was erected by King Anizham Tirunal in the 18th century. Made entirely of teak wood taken from the nearby forests, the flagpole was covered in gold foils after it was carved. A figurine of Garuda, the divine vehicle of Lord Vishnu is carved at the top. The specialty of this pole was that the teak wood brought from the forests was not allowed to touch the ground during its entire journey to the temple.

The nine doors of the temple represent the nine orifices in the human body. The seven storeys of the main east-facing entrance's gopuram represent the seven worlds as believed by the Hindus. The first three stories of this gopuram has intricate carvings that depicted the 10 incarnations of Lord Vishnu. The entry to the other fourth storey of the gopuram is restricted. All the other entrances are simple double-storied padippuras made in the typical Kerala architectural style.

Mr. Raman then continued, "As far as the water resources are concerned, there are number of them. Padmatheertham is one of the oldest water bodies in the city of Trivandrum. Some people even believe that Padmatheertham hides an underwater tunnel, but where it leads to is unknown."

By now, Vijay was sure that Mr. Raman was a sea of knowledge about the temple and its history. He had to tap and churn out every possible bit of information from the old man.

The two men never realized how engrossed they had been in the conversation. They soon reached Mr. Raman's house. The house looked as old as the man who lived in it. The surrounding was deserted. Vijay and the team of experts were supposed to unlock the secret vaults a day after, which meant he had only one day to gather as much as information as possible under the cover of a tourist. He did not want to let go this opportunity. Hence, he did not deny the invitation for a cup of coffee from the old man.

Upon entering the house, Vijay offered to prepare coffee for both of them while the old man caught his breath after the long walk from the temple. On the way to the kitchen, Vijay had a quick glimpse of the house. The one thing he could notice was, that Mr. Raman led a very mediocre life in a very small house. The house had a book in every nook and corner, and many hand written papers too. Vijay assumed that Mr. Raman himself wrote the papers.

He had a hunch that Mr. Raman's knowledge hasn't received the recognition it truly deserved. He had never had the audience with whom he hoped to share his vast knowledge. Vijay chose to gamble on these very emotions.

Vijay knew it wouldn't be difficult for him to tingle the old man's desire to have a listener as keen as himself. But then he had to appear as natural as possible because he didn't want the old man to know his true identity yet. Sipping the coffee, Vijay asked if the coffee had enough sugar. Mr. Raman nodded in affirmation and asked Vijay if he was used to looking after himself. Vijay said yes, as he had to take care of his sick grandfather for many years.

Pointing at the papers on the floor, he began the second leg of the conversation. He asked if the papers all over the house were part of some book he was writing?

Suddenly, the smile on Mr. Raman's face disappeared. The old man nodded in affirmation with a grim face. He said they are the left overs of the research he was doing on the historical temples in the country. As a historian, he wanted to bring the rich, ancient cultural heritage of the land to light. He had dedicated his life for this cause.

He was highly motivated towards this goal until the day he realized how much the authorities and the so-called citizens of this great country cared about the lost heritage. In frustration, he had burnt almost all of his work. It was such a moment of foolish rage that made him destroy a lifetime of his work.

He had lost himself in depression. Till the Lord himself in the form of a kid came to his rescue and forced him to read out the Gita. It was a transformation for him and that was when he decided to read the holy book every day at the temple and survive with the little money he earned from this exercise.

It was just a couple of weeks ago, a young boy from the nearby government college came to him seeking some guidance for one of his assignments. In spite of telling him multiple times not to bother him, the boy kept returning, requesting for help.

Mr. Raman admitted he had no idea, how the boy had found the whereabouts of him. Finally, when he had no option but to give in to the boy's persistence, he did some research for the boy. While looking for the information the boy wanted, his house turned into a mess. However, strangely enough, when he had found the information the boy was looking for, he hadn't turned up for it yet. Given Mr. Raman's age, he had lost the patience to put the house back in shape. But he was happy to admit the boy had rekindled the love he had towards historic research.

The enthusiasm on Mr. Raman's face was enough proof for Vijay to understand, how willing he was to share what he knew. Vijay was on the lookout for this very opportunity. He said he had inherited his fondness for Indian mythology and history from his grandfather. But what he had heard about Sree Anantha Padmanabha Swamy Temple were stories that were only passed on to him through word of mouth.

He would consider it his honour, if he could get to listen to a few stories from Mr. Raman himself. The qualities of good listening and keen observation, which Vijay had exhibited, were some of the qualities the old man wished for in a research junior,if he ever had one.

Hence, when he was requested to share his knowledge about the temple with such humility the old man could not deny. He folded his hands in complete devotion to the lord and began.

CHAPTER 3

The Anantha Padmanabha Swamy Temple at Trivandrum has been mentioned in many Hindu texts, including some of the extant Puranas and even the Mahabharata. The temple has been mentioned in many works of the Tamil Sangam Literature, which has been dated back by many historians between 500 B.C and 300 A.D.

Mr. Raman began his story. The legend of this wondrous temple areas follows. Sage Vilvamangalathu Swamiyar lived near present-day Kasargod, close to the Ananthapuram Temple. It is believed that Lord Vishnu answered his fervent prayers for a darshan by appearing as a mischievous little boy before him. As part of his childish demeanour, the little boy is believed to have defiled the Lord's idol. The sage was livid at this and being ignorant of the child's true identity, chased away the boy. When he realized his mistake, he searched high and low for the boy and finally was inspired by a mother's angry words toward her erring child. The mother seemed to have said that she would throw him into the Ananthakadu (or the forest of eternity). Hearing these words, the sage found his way to this forest in search of the Lord in guise of the boy.

In this forest, the sage witnessed the boy merging into an iluppai tree, popularly known as the Indian Butter tree. This tree came crashing down and is took on the shape of a Reclining Vishnu or the Anantha Sayana Moorthi. But this idol was nearly 8 miles long with the head in Tiruvollam, the navel in Trivandrum and the feet in Thrippadapuram. Begging the Lord for forgiveness for his harsh treatment toward the boy, the sage asked him to reduce the size of the edifice so that it can be seen in its entirety. The Lord obliged. The place where Sage Vilvamangalathu Swamiyar got a darshan of Lord Anantha Padmanabha Swamy, belonged to a couple by name Karuva Potti and Koopakkara Potti. A temple was built with the help of the local king and some Namboodiri Brahmins, and Koopakkara Potti was appointed the Tantri of this temple.

Vijay expressed delight on listening to the mercy of the Lord on the sage and the manner Mr. Raman narrated it by folding his hands and bowing to the Almighty.

He added that now he understood why his grandfather wanted to breathe his last in one of the most pious places on earth. The old historian nodded in agreement to Vijay's grandfather's sentiments. Then he began to explain why many believed this adobe of the lord is believed to be a Mahakshetram (Great temple).

Mr. Raman seemed almost teleported to the time he was narrating about and that is exactly the state of mind Vijay wanted him to be in. Now was the time when Vijay had to choose his words very carefully. It was at that moment, when he had to ask the questions that mattered to him.

He began by saying that it was so unfortunate for such a pious place to be highlighted for all the wrong reasons. Vijay earnestly asked Mr. Raman whether he really think that there were invaluable treasures hidden in the secret vaults in the temple. The old man allowed himself a wry smile.

Then he continued, this time with a question. "Why do you think the Mughals, the French, the Portuguese and the English got attracted to India? Because India had immense riches, isn't it? History tells you, Mahmud of Ghazni, the Turkish invader, invaded India 17 times attracted by the wealth of the land. Temples were one of the hideouts where rulers across the land used to hide their treasure.

Hence the possibility of a treasure being hidden somewhere in the temple is quite bright." Having known the history of the royal family of Trivandrum, Mr. Raman continued, "In centuries past, Maharajas had performed a ceremony in which they weighed the princes approaching adulthood, and donating to the temple an equivalent weight in gold.

In that case, the then temple caretakers must have kept that wealth safe somewhere. No one could be foolish enough to keep such wealth open under the stars, to allow anyone to loot it without breaking a drop of sweat."

Vijay asked again how Mr. Raman was so confident that the temple hid immeasurable riches in its womb. The old man pointed to an old thing in one of the two shelves, which looked like nothing more than a bunch of torn pages hanging together. But it was a book according to the old man. He asked Vijay to bring it to him. He the opened the book to a chapter on the temple and read aloud a sentence that he had underlined, "A cellar underneath the shrine secures the temple jewels."

Vijay still looked uncertain. It was then when he was asked to retrieve another book from which the old man read out a passage. It read that the local government borrowed money from the temple way back in 1855 when it faced financial difficulties. Doesn't this mean that the temple must have had access to plenty of wealth?

Mr. Raman continued. He said that he was not accusing the royal family or anyone for mismanagement of temple riches. It is possible that most members of the current and previous generation of the royal family might not even know about the treasure hidden in the temple.

Those people who are or were aware of the existence of the untold wealth lying under the temple, considered it divine and not meant for digging up and using it for other purposes. Unlike the Western thought that relies on closure of all elements to feel content and happy, Indian thought is based on the belief that there are many inexplicable things in the world that cannot be explained.

Accepting their mystery and divinity is not just a simple principle for contentment. It is believed to be good for the society and the world at large to let those mysteries remain unexplained and unexplored. Wealth stored in the temples of India is not given any monetary value. It is treated with respect and love as a large part of this wealth represent the payment made in kind by believers when their desires have been fulfilled by the Lord.

Vijay wanted to know more. He asked the old man how the temple amassed such great. The old man asked Vijay to bring another book, which was about the royal family of Trivandrum and began reading one of the chapters.

The region of Travancore, later known as Trivandrum, was ruled by a cruel king in the 18th century who conquered many kingdoms and brought in a lot of wealth. This king earned the wrath and anger of many rivals. The prominent ones being a set of kings calling themselves the lords of the eight houses.

These men hatched an assassination plot against the cruel Maharaja of Travancore, which was supposed to be carried out during one of the festivals at Sree Padmanabha Swamy Temple. An old man who got wind of this plot warned the king about it.

On the fateful day, the king came to the festival with a huge retinue of soldiers and put down many rebels. He killed the men, sold off the women and children, and seized their wealth.

In an attempt to repent against these cruel crimes, the Maharaja of Travancore proclaimed that the wealth seized from these rebels will be given to Lord Padmanabha Swamy. Moreover, he dedicated his entire kingdom along with all the wealth to the Lord.

Mr. Raman added that this wealth was locked up beneath the temple. But it wasn't clear what happened to the riches over the centuries.

Most of the historians did not focus on the wealth because they believed that investigating this aspect was not part of their job.

There is no rocket science involved to understand that the royal family had very few confidants. But it was once rumoured among locals that, a few hundred years ago, the loyalty of one of the chief priests earned himself the trust of the then maharaja to such an extent that the priest was allowed to pass on the royal secrets to his next generation, provided he had the same level of trust the maharaja had on him.

Vijay sprang up with a question "Doesn't anyone ask that priest's family about those secrets?" The old man replied, "They could if they had lived." Vijay again asked Raman with a confused look on his face what he meant.

The old man said as fate had it, the chosen priest's family had been reduced to an old man who had inherited the appointment as chief priest and a young grandson. Unfortunately, the chief priest was found dead in a fire accident and no one knows what happened to his grandchild.

Hearing this, an alarm rang in Vijay's mind. Was Mr. Raman talking about his grandfather? Did this old man know anything about the alleged treasure? Was it the reason of his mysterious death?

Numerous uncertainties started racing in Vijay's mind. Was he going to realize the greatest of his fears? Was his beloved grandfather going to be branded as a cheat, a traitor? Were all the sacrifices he had made, life risks he had taken were to be disregarded as fake?

But before Mr. Raman could notice the anxiety building on Vijay's face, he was alert enough to regain his composure and change the topic. He asked Mr. Raman, what did he think should be done with the wealth, if any was indeed found hidden in the temple.

Mr. Raman replied if there indeed is treasure hidden in the temple, then the people and the authorities must know about it. So that it can be well protected and utilized for the development and growth of the nation at large. Unfortunately, many wouldn't agree with me in this country. Vijay was indeed impressed by the old man's radical thinking, but also was relieved that he was not caught.

The two men had lost track of time in their conversation. It was well over midnight when Vijay saw his watch and realized it was high time he let the old man rest. But before he left, he requested Mr. Raman to be mindful of the temple raid by the expert team sent by the Supreme Court and hence, he better stay home the next morning.

Word in the city had spread like wild fire that the temple would remain closed for the mass as the authorities expected public rage in the city regarding the raid at the temple.

The next morning was June 30, 2011. It was around 9 a.m. The sun was beating down with all its fury, as if it wanted to melt the people who go against the will of the Supreme Lord. The expert team, along with the local police and team of firefighters led by the former director of the National Museum tried to enter the temple from the east, where they were not allowed to enter.

The authorities handed over the orders from top court to the head of the royal family, Marthanda Varma III, according to which they had the authority to search every corner of the temple. The team was reluctantly allowed inside the temple. They were accompanied by Sundaraajan, a historian and an important member of the public committee, who filed the case of funds mismanagement by the temple authorities. Sundaraajan knew that there were six vaults, out of which four were regularly accessed as they held the ornaments for the various festivals of the temple. These four vaults were situated in the southern side of the temple. However, Sundaraajan led the investigation team to the other side—the Northern side, where the Ayyappa shrine was located. Sundaraajan, along with the expert committee was accompanied with a chief priest and few temple assistants.

He started looking for a secret door or some kind of entrance to the two secret vaults near the Ayyappa temple. He felt his hands on all the walls of the Sanctum Sanctorum, but couldn't find anything that seemed to open any door that led them to the vaults.

He even tried feeling the floor by going down on his knees for some clue, but his effort was in vain.

Sundaraajan was behaving like a cat sniffing for a mouse. Seeing him, Vijay asked,

"Are you sure you are looking at the right place?"

"Yes. According to my research, the vaults are under this Ayyappa temple. That is why I am looking for a secret entrance that will lead us there."

Vijay entered the Ayyappa shrine and began to look inside for some breakthrough. He too felt his hands on the walls inside. He looked even at the back of the Ayyappa idol, but didn't find anything.

Suddenly, he noticed that one of the walls had a huge closet. He slid inside the closet to see that if housed an idol or not. He saw the temple deity on a broad wooden plank. This deity was brought out on festive occasions only.

Beneath the plank were stairs leading down. Sundaraajan looked at everyone with a sense of achievement in his eyes. All the observers were astonished by the presence of the passage under the plank. Vijay wondered why no one thought of lifting the plank all these years. Led by Vijay with his torch, the men began to descend the stairs.

The steps led to the two vaults located in one side of a long rectangular room. The observers were able to find the keys that opened the metal grille doors of one of the vaults. Behind this, they found another wooden door, which they were able to open with one of the keys they had with them. Behind this wooden door was another iron door that had two paintings of cobras etched on it. This door, strangely, had no bolts, no nuts, no keyholes, nothing that could be turned to open it. At this moment the chief priest rushed to protest, the forceful opening of this door. He thundered, "This door is believed to be fixed to the secret chamber with the Naga Bandham or Naga Paasam mantras (sacred rituals to protect something against evil) by then Siddha Purashas who lived during the reign of King Marthanda Varma in the 16th century."

Such doors can only be opened by reciting a powerful Garuda Mantra by highly knowledgeable and scholarly mantrikas. There is no other way of opening this door.

Presently, there was no learned soil either in India or in the entire materialistic world, who is knowledgeable enough to recite this mantra, as taught in the Vedas. Even if sadhus who knew this sacred mantra are alive, they are beyond human contact as they have achieved the higher plane of knowledge and do not find any reason to get back to mundane life.

If anyone tried to force open the door using manmade technologies, then it is prophesied that catastrophes are bound to happen.

At that point of time, a few of the team members got influenced by the priest, maybe, because they were god-fearing people. Vijay saw traces of fear on their faces and just before he could utter word, one of them spotted a snake insignia. It was several feet long. No one had seen an insignia of such a huge length in their entire life and this set the cat among the pigeons.

A few of the team members now looked uncertain about opening the vault. Sunderaajan and Vijay did not want to let go this opportunity, hence Vijay suggested opening the other cellar a few metres away.

Once again, they unlocked two outer doors—one of metal and the other of wood. They found themselves in a little room with a big rectangular slab placed in the middle. Five men had to work for over 30 minutes before the slab was lifted and moved aside. Leading from the hole that was covered by the slab was a dark, narrow passage, just wide enough for one adult to pass through, leading down through a set of stairs.

The firefighters pumped in oxygen into this descending passage so that people could safely walk down without fear. At the bottom of the descending stairs was the sixth vault. There was absolutely darkness except for a sliver of light coming out of the vault.

What the men saw in the vault looked like stars glittering in a night sky, when there is no moon, except that what glittered were not stars but countless gems and diamonds. It looked like these sparkling gems and precious stones were kept in wooden boxes. But over time, the wooden boxes turned to dust leaving all the precious stones lying on the floor, giving the entire room the appearance of a clear black night sky glittering with numerous little stars.

There were bangles, chains and necklaces of a few feet long—all designed to fit the long idol of the Lord in the temple. It took 15 men all day, to haul everything upstairs, from the vault, for inspection.

Looking at such wealth being carried out of the vault, all the observers including the members of the expert committee, were amazed. But they were honest and professional enough to realize, their role was only to report the findings of the vault.

In the next couple of days, media from all over the world was in Trivandrum to know more about the treasure. Majority of the locals exhibited hostile reactions, saying that the government must let the treasure that belongs to the temple stay as it is.

Reporters and media from all over the country and the world landed at the temple to cover the spectacular news. There were many protesters in the crowd too. Most of the protesters were zealous devotees of the Lord, who worried that the wealth belonging to their God will be taken away.

Sundaraajan was the main target for these protesters. Calling him derogatory names like thief and looter of the Lord's wealth, these people screamed in anger against the man. Strangely enough, about a fortnight later, on July 16th to be precise, Sundaraajan took ill with a fever that no one thought much of at that time. But that night he laid down on his bed never to wake up again.

Speculation around the mysterious death of the man, believed by devotees, to be responsible to committing sacrilege, spread like wild fire all through the country and the world. People believed that he fell victim to the curse of the cobras.

But Vijay believed that what had to be done, had to be done. After a couple of weeks, the findings of the first vault were well documented and sent to the authorities. The temple authorities were asked to get the things found in the vault to their original place.

In a couple of days, Vijay headed to the Kowdiar Palace, where he was to meet princess Laxmi Bai of the royal family. The Kowdiar was old and dilapidated. Yet,it held a royal aura aided by the huge structure that held 106 rooms—all furnished with teak wood that enhanced the sense of opulence even further. Intricate carpets, despite being dusty and uncared for, and marvellous oil paintings that brought alive stories from the Hindu epics, made the palace even more appealing to the common man.

Vijay's visit to meet Princess Laxmi Bai was to try and convince her to speak to the local and explain the importance of having to open the 6th vault. Vijay believed that a supportive word from a member of the royal family would help his team do a better job.

The princess said to Vijay, "We consider ourselves slaves to the Lord. While a master can choose to abandon his slave, a slave can never abandon his master. And so it is with us too." She further added, "I believe that the 6th vault is connected to the sanctum sanctorum through a powerfully spiritual connection, which can be felt only by those who are very fortunate. Disturbing this mysterious connection is not good for anyone. The cobra paintings on the door stand testimony to the misfortune that begets anyone who tries to disturb the vault."

Vijay asked what would happen if the energy was disturbed. The princess narrated to him the story of another Indian temple which housed a levitating idol. It was a stunning piece of idol that mesmerized worshipers who felt its power very strongly. However, this hovering idol came crashing down when workers began some kind of renovation work and that beautiful spirit was lost forever. The princess feared that some similar disaster would affect the people who believed in Lord Anantha Padmanabha Swamy if Vault B, that is the sixth vault, was disturbed. She feared that some disaster would strike the city of Trivandrum too.

A few days later, Vijay met the head of the royal family, Marthanda Varma III at Pattom Palace—a huge, white, wooden structure and red-tiled roof, with the same request. The old man was vehement in his opposition to open the vault, as he believed that all that talk of immense wealth in vault B were simply baseless. A group of astrologers were called for consultation. They held a 4-day ceremony called as Devaprasnam to determine the will of the Lord.

A young boy was found to do the needful work. He was given a bath and purified. He was made to sit at a clean place and eight items were placed in front of him, which included a mirror, a lamp, a piece of cloth, betel leaves, grains of rice, the Bhagvat Gita and an ancient gold coin. The astrologers sprinkled some sacred rice powder to draw a chart. They gave the boy 108 conch shells and asked him to arrange it on the chart.

While the boy was arranging the shells, the astrologers prayed for the right message to be sent through the boy. After this elaborate ceremony, it was concluded that the Lord was not happy to allow the opening of vault B. This, combined with the ominous death of Sundaraajan, had instilled a sense of fear in all. The Supreme Court, under pressure from the people, had to put off the opening of vault B in fear of violent retaliation from the devotees.

Vijay tried his best to convince the court to reverse its decision. But his efforts were in vain. As somewhere deep within, he also wanted to find if his grandfather's death was related to the secret of the temple vault. Anyone but an intelligence officer would have given into the temptation of breaking into the vault. But Vijay was a trained officer and he was supposed to follow protocol.

The kind of missions he was constantly sent to, he hardly could do much about either finding the truth behind the last vault of the temple or the truth behind his grandfather's involvement in safeguarding any secret of the temple.

CHAPTER 4

Vijay was brought back to reality this time by a sound on his fax machine. The fax was from the Bureau—a set of documents he might need on his new assignment. It mainly contained a copy of few pages a book called Travancore: A guide book for the visitor, authored by Emily Gilchrist Hatch.

In her book, Hatch wrote that a huge number of cobras that seemed to lay in wait for any intruders scared off a group of people who tried to open the vault in 1931. However, another fax of an earlier audit report said that this vault was opened and no serpents were found. It was now up to Vijay to throw some light on this confusing matter.

Vijay's mind was clouded with various thoughts, but something from within told him that the exploration he was part of this time, would immortalize him in History. He also felt that he would also find something that would help him find out, if his family was the one who was the confidant of the royal family. Just for a brief moment, he just hoped that he doesn't discover some bitter truth about his ancestors. He did feel vulnerable for a while.

Then, his intellect reminded him, what he had learnt in his training, how much bitter the truth could be, it has to be brought to light someday.

The next evening, Vijay including the expert team had reached Trivandrum to similar emotions from the public that they were subject to five years ago. But this time around, the local authorities were better prepared. The route from the airport to the government guest house was off by the local police. The city of Trivandrum was on high alert.

That was one of the longest nights of Vijay's life. It was after a long time that he felt so restless; he was like a cat on hot roof. The needles of the clock seemed to be stuck, refusing to budge an inch. The nervous energy in Vijay did not allow him to sleep even for a minute.

The next morning, the team was dressed in the local attire,a dhoti and a shirt. Vijay and his junior Akshay, a new recruit, carried a cloth handbag in which they carried high-resolution cameras and also managed to hide an 'Austrian Glock 19', a pistol made of plastic used by NSG's and Para commandos. As they suspected a public outrage and in such a scenario, they could use the weapon to scare away the mob.

The team, this time led by Vijay, followed by the local police, a team of firefighters and black smith to cut open the iron door with the portrait of cobras. On the way to the temple, they saw mobs holding banners and shouting slogans against them. The temple was surrounded by a crowd of devotees,although it was closed for all of them.

Like the previous time, the head of the royal family who waited for the team since early morning was handed the orders from the court. As per the order,the team was free to break open the vault in question. A couple of minutes later, a contingent of 15 men including the head of the royal family reached the vault.

"Fear the rage of the Lord; don't make him angry. You will open the doors of hell not only for yourself but all of us." The chief priest roared. This was his last attempt to prevent the team to force open the iron door.

"I have been asked to open this door and that I will do it at any cost. The amount of gold behind these six doors could solve money-related problems in this country. But you will not allow that to happen. You will rather decorate those 12008 lifeless stones with the gold and other valuables."

Vijay stepped forward, looked into the priest's eyes and said, "I am trying really hard to hold my temper, so don't test my patience. As far as opening the door of hell is concerned, I don't give a damn about it."

Vijay's cold, steely firm eyes caught the chief priest off guard. He hadn't expected such a response. Vijay too realised he might have said a word or two more. He immediately mellowed down his voice and said, "Sir, I completely understand your fear and concern, but you don't have to be scared. We have enough proof that this door was opened earlier and nothing happened. Hence, I request you to cooperate with us."

The chief priest stepped aside and allowed the blacksmith to gear up the automatic saw to cut open the iron door. Seconds later, the saw began roaring to do its job. But the blacksmith wasn't—he was dead scared to lend his hand in opening the door. Literally trembling and perspiring, given a chance he would have fled from the temple. The local police had forcefully brought him to make way for the expert team.

Vijay noticed the blacksmith's fear and took the tool from him. He asked him to leave and not to worry about his tools. They would reach him safely, as soon as their work was done.

The blacksmith fell to Vijay's feet and said, "Sir, all I care about now is my life. I have dependents on me. I cannot afford to die or become a dependent myself." He continued "These priests are well versed in mantras (spells) to please the Lord. All you rich people are capable of taking care of your families without you being around. But if the Lord unleashes his fury, there is no one to protect me or my family. I will be grateful to you forever for your mercy on me."

Vijay patted his back and let him go. He restarted the saw and was about to begin cutting the door. Before starting on the door, he wanted to make sure that there was no other way to open it. If the 2014 reports were to be true, he suspected signs of metal damage due to repair of the door. But first he asked everyone, except the royal family members and his team, to vacate the area. Everyone, except Vijay and his assistant, present there were petrified when they saw Vijay touching and feeling the door—especially when they saw him touch the cobra portraits on the door.

Vijay first felt all the corners of the door and then the snake portrait on the left of the door, but found nothing unusual in it. Then he felt the portrait on the right. The moment he touched the eye of the snake, he realized the portrait was not carved just to showcase the talent of the sculptor or to scare trespassers away.

Yes. It did that as well because they were so well carved and ornate that the snakes seemed as scary and fierce as a real giant cobra could be. His keen observation made him realise that the eye of the snake was hollow, something like a button.

Akshay, who was closely watching Vijay, noticed that he had found something very interesting. Vijay stuck his ear on the door and pressed the eye of the cobra as if he pressed a button, he heard a latch unfasten itself. Immediately the two halves of the door started to slide in their respective sides. With a creaking noise, the legendary door opened. Everyone present there was dumbfounded at the wonderful combination of architecture and engineering of the ancient times, but only to see a huge wooden door,which was locked. Vijay asked the head of the royal family for the key, which would open the lock on the wooden door. Unfortunately, he was told by the current head of the royal family that after the death of Marthanda Varma III in 2013, not much attention was paid to these antique keys. What the current head was aware was that there were couple of antique keys well-kept in the auspicious prayer room in his palace.

Vijay asked him to get those keys immediately. A temple staff, accompanied by the local police constable, was sent to the palace for the keys. They had to wait for about 30 minutes for the keys to arrive, as the distance from the temple to the Pattom Palace is almost four kilometres one way. The head of the royal family asked, "What if the rumours I have been hearing come true?"

Vijay asked, "What do you hear?"

He replied, "One hears the gurgling of water, the hissing of snakes on the other side of the door if one listens at the door."

Akshay immediately put his ear on the door, but couldn't hear anything. Vijay then comforted the head of the royal family and said, "Don't worry sir. If there was a giant snake in there, we would have seen more signs than just an insignia. The insignia we saw five years ago could have come from anywhere. A wild snake might have entered the temple from the woods, and we saw the insignia on the very day of the raid."

"As far as water is concerned, do you hear gurgling of water in there? Where does it flow? All the water resources in or around the temple premises are stagnant. There is no place the water could flow to."

As he finished his sentence, the police constable and temple staff returned and handed four antique keys to Vijay.

As he inserted the first key to unlock the door, there was expectancy in everyone; an expectancy of a multiple headed serpent's hiss, raising its hood, may be even spit fire, or somehow destroy everything that is around it. The first key didn't work. Neither did the second nor the third. Everyone, except Vijay, thought the fourth key too won't open the door. He instructed his assistant to arm himself with his weapon and be very alert.

As he pushed open the door, Vijay quickly pulled out his Glock and a torch. He was the first to tiptoe with bent knees into the vault. The others were instructed to stay out till he signalled. He couldn't stand straight as the ceiling was too low.

The vault seemed similar to the vault opened in 2011, but a little smaller in size—approximately 12 by 15 square feet in dimension. It was filled with something solid and there was very little space to walk. Vijay switched on the torch and there he saw nothing but gold.

There were ten statues signifying the incarnations of lord Vishnu. There were few wooden benches on which were kept tens of sets of solid gold blocks in pyramid shape. There also were a couple of huge diamond studded bows and loads of antique ornaments. Vijay estimated the worth of this vault in billions.

He was not interested in the gold. His first priority was to make sure the vault was safe for people to enter. Once he was sure that there was no danger, he called a few temple helpers and asked them to carefully carry each thing out of the vault, so that each thing could be carefully documented.

While this was being done, amidst all the gold, Vijay's eye caught a mid-sized metal box. Vijay kept his weapon in his handbag and went to have a closer look at it. It was one of the most unglamorous boxes he had seen in his life. The box had turned black in colour due to the oxidation of the alloy. It was rectangular, with a semi-circular lid on its top. The fact that such a box was kept amidst things that shined, intrigued him.

He noticed the box had a latch and was locked. The lock had been wound with numerous red threads. Vijay knew Hindus interpret *kalava* (red thread) as a symbol of protection. It is believed to defend the wearer against everything—from enemies to natural disasters or any other form of evil. The color red is extremely significant in the Hindu faith. It symbolizes both purity and—as the color of the deity Shakti—prowess. Other Hindu deities that wear red often represent bravery, generosity or security. Vijay was curious to know what was being protected in that metal box so religiously.

On the other hand, there was the seal of the royal family of Travancore on these threads. It was the image of two elephants guarding the imperial Sree Padmanabha's Shanku (Conch) in its imperial crest. Vijay had an intuition that the box hid something much more valuable than anything that was found in any of the six vaults in the temple. He was also sure that if not the current or previous generation of the royals, the older generations knew about what was being hidden in the box.

Vijay lifted the box to one of the benches and knew that it held something heavy. Then he began unwinding the red threads that were wound on the lock. Once he had removed the last strand of the thread on the lock, he stepped out of the vault and asked the head of royal family if he knew anything about the alloy box and its key? "No!" The answer was prompt. He then started to look for any cutting instrument in the tool set of the blacksmith and found a hacksaw blade. He checked on its sharpness and took it back into the vault.

Vijay began cutting down the lock on the alloy box. It was not difficult. After seeing so much wealth in this as well as the other vault, an automatic excitement was bound to build within Vijay. But as soon as the lock was cut, the latch opened and the lid lifted, all the excitement built fizzed out in an anti-climax. He expected to see something spectacular, but what he saw was a most ordinary ear then pot.

But this rang umpteen bells and raised numerous questions in his mind. The greatest question being— why an earthen pot was secured this way with wealth of such immeasurable quantity and value?

He saw a plain, colour less earthen pot, under which lay a wooden plank of the length of the pot, which was a couple of feet long. At the mouth of the pot was a plank, which was of the width of the base of the pot and just deep enough to hold the base of the pot. Vijay made the pot stand in the box, for a second he speculated not inserting his hand into the pot. He suspected some danger in it. Then he thought that it was only one way to find out. He put his hand in the pot but found nothing.

Vijay wondered why the short wide plank was kept with the pot. By then, he knew that nothing in the temple was just what it looked like and nothing was in its place without any rhyme or reason. Though he didn't understand the actual purpose of the short, wide plank, he knew that such a plank could be used to keep the pot. But before doing so he did check if the base of the pot would allow the pot to stand stable. He didn't find anything unusual, hence very carefully placed the pot on the short, wide plank.

What he did notice was the image of the sun engraved along with Aum Aim Hreem Kleemen graved around the pot. These were basic alphabets of the Vedic language, in the original script of Devanagari, which is the source of most Indian languages. Vijay had no idea what these engraved images on the pot meant. He asked the head of the royal family if he or any of his family members knew anything about the pot or the engraving on it. But they didn't. Yet Vijay knew for sure that Ancient Hindu scriptures describe Om or Aum as the primordial sound from which the Universe was created. He did not know much about the rest of the other alphabets.

Vijay felt there must be more to this and continued to explore the box. He found nothing on the walls of the box. He lifted the longer wooden plank on which the pot was placed. There, he saw an engraved copper plate. He picked it up to have a closer look at what was engraved on it.

Though he knew copper does not rust or decay and can survive indefinitely, yet he was amazed to know that the engraving in the box had survived for so many centuries without any sign of oxidization.

Vijay identified the language of the engraving on the plate. It was in original Devanagari script; he had learnt reading Devanagari during his training of being a priest. But he thought it was better if experts like the former director of the national museum, who was an archaeologist, have a closer look at the engraving. Vijay was hoping that the old eyes would be able to shed some light on the mystery of the pot. The old man agreed that the language of engraving was indeed Devanagari.

He also said that metal or alloy engraving was used to document very rare and important information till as late as the early twentieth century. Then it lost its popularity and became limited to forms of security printing. The old man asserted, "whatever this engraving is related to must be of great value. That is the reason the letter has been engraved on copper. So that it could stand the test of time."

He then began reading out the content of the engraving. It was a letter from the King of Banaras, Udit Narayan Singh Sahib Bahadur, to the King of Travancore, Karthika Thirunal Rama Varma.

The archaeologist translated the engraving and read - Your Majesty! O great King Karthika Thirunal Rama Varma. I, the ruler of Banaras Udit Narayan Singh Sahib Bahadur pay you my greatest respects and hoping that this letter reaches you in the greatest of spirits. I have great regard towards the knowledge that you not only possess about righteousness, but also your diligence in practising it to the best of your ability. Hence, you are known as the 'Dharma Raja' (righteous king). Along with this letter, I am sending this earthen pot to keep in your possession. This pot has great mystic powers hidden within it which, if used constructively, can change lives for the better. But if used otherwise, has the potential to destroy it. It is because of the righteous deeds performed by you and your ancestors, that your kingdom has been blessed with great visionary minds.

My kingdom is prone to invasions from foreign powers and hence, this pot isn't safe in my custody.

There lives a great astrologer and sage in your kingdom, Shankar Narayan Namboodiri. He knows all about the legendary prowess of this pot. I request you to invite him to your presence and be advised of the legendary attributes of it. With great hope and belief, that you will do everything necessary to safeguard this pot, I make you its custodian."

The letter ended with the royal seal of King of Banaras. After hearing the content engraved on the copper plate, a sense of excitement, curiosity and also fear, to a great extent, engulfed most of the people present there. The old archaeologist slowly went to the pot and very carefully it picked up to have a closer look. He looked and felt the engravings on the pot. He tried to put all his experience together and relate his knowledge to the letter and the pot.

"Do you know anything about what you read now sir?", asked Vijay, very eagerly. But the old man looked at Vijay and said, "The names mentioned on the copper plate sound familiar. As far as I know and if my memory serves me right, Udit Narayan Singh Sahib Bahadur ruled Banaras in the 18th century and Karthika Thirunal Rama Varma was the King of Travancore during the same period. That means this scripture is at least couple of centuries old."

"As per the content on the scripture, this pot holds a very potent secret within itself. But there is no clue as to how to reveal it whatsoever, except for a name of a legendary astrologer. I suppose there isn't a way to find a man or his bloodline, who lived two centuries ago."

Vijay agreed in his mind, but didn't acknowledge it. As he knew it wouldn't be easy tracking down the astrologer, he simply kept mum. He recalled Mr. Raman telling him about the chief priest who served at the temple two decades ago. The old man had also mentioned the chief priest might have known the greatest secrets of the royal family of Travancore. What Vijay was wondering was whether his grandfather knew the secret that Shankar Narayan Namboodiri knew? And if so, does Vijay himself share the bloodline of the legendary astrologer?

He realized that there was only one person who could guide him at this juncture. That was the old historian he had met five years ago, Mr. Raghuraman. But before he could go to him, he had to be sure that he got all the required information and supporting documents required to complete his report. He had to make sure that every finding was perfectly photographed and documented. Vijay searched frantically to find a tool or resource to make the engraving brighter in the photograph.

The archaeologist came to Vijay and said, "I think I know what you are looking for." He handed Vijay a piece of crayon. Vijay appreciated the old man's observation and carefully began rewriting on the engraving to make it brighter. He then nailed the copper sheet to the wooden plan and asked Akshay to click a clear picture of the pot and the engraved copper plate. Vijay himself clicked a picture of the pot and the engraving on his smart phone.

After photographing every finding of the vault, the temple staff was requested to arrange everything back in the vault as before. The doors were securely closed. Vijay led the team outside the temple premises where they met a sea of media professionals from all over the world. They wanted to know if the vault was opened in the first place and if it was, what was found inside it?

Vijay exempted himself and the team from answering any questions from the media by saying,

"It is obvious from everyone in the team returning alive that there was no danger in the vault. My team will be submitting the report to the top officials and the top court of the country will declare what was found in the vault."

Akshay was instructed to prepare a detailed report on the temple raid and most importantly, add recommendations on security arrangements. This was mainly because Vijay was aware how modern technology could be ill-used to steal the treasure found and get away with it. Then no one knew where Vijay disappeared.

He remembered the route to Mr. Raman's house vividly, though it had been five years since he had visited the place. But he was unsure about how he was to reveal his identity to the old man. Would Mr. Raman help him after he gets to know who he really was? Would he be able to understand that as an intelligence officer, Vijay was not authorized to reveal his identity. Would he understand that although lying about his grandfather's death to the old man wasn't right, it was ethical in the larger context?

With all such apprehensions, Vijay reached in front of the old man's doorstep. He realised the door wasn't locked—he saw it ajar. Vijay thought that since it was noon, Mr. Raman might be having a nap and, by mistake, had left the door open. He felt it would not be a wise idea to wake him up. Vijay's nervousness increased. He told himself that he would comeback in the evening and talk to the old man.

He turned his back and was about to leave. That is exactly when he heard someone coughing frantically from inside the house and a tumbler fall. Could Mr. Raman be seriously sick, unattended, or even on his death bed? And is it the reason he is unable to open the door? That the old man may not have had access to food or water for more than a couple of days also crossed Vijay's mind. Living alone in a deserted house might have added to his woes.

Vijay called out the old man's name aloud, but there was no response. He pushed the door open but couldn't see Mr. Raman in the drawing room. He then looked in the adjacent room where he found the old man lying unconscious on the floor. His head was bleeding because of a wound he had from the fall. Vijay rushed to him and tied his handkerchief to Mr. Raman's wound. While doing so, Vijay noticed that Mr. Raman was running high temperature and needed immediate medical attention. Vijay called the 24-hour ambulance service without wasting a second and got the historian admitted to a hospital. In a couple of hours he was diagnosed with a viral fever. The condition of the old man had worsened because the man hadn't eaten anything for two or more days.

The intelligence officer took it upon himself to stay in the hospital and be the old man's caretaker. For reasons unknown, Vijay sensed a kind off attachment towards the old man. The next couple of days he stayed by Mr. Raman's side. When the old man regained consciousness and opened his eyes, the first person he saw was the doctor.

As soon as Mr. Raman had gained conscious, he asked the doctor about how did he reach the hospital? Who admitted him? The doctor said, "You should be grateful to this man!" The doctor was pointing at Vijay, who had just entered the room carrying the medicines for the old man. Vijay gently patted the old man's shoulder and asked him, "How're you doing, Mr. Raman?"

The old man nodded his head with a weak smile, probably meaning to say that he felt better. Vijay asked him to rest and assured him that he will be around in case he was needed. He was about to leave the room, closing the door behind him, when he heard his name being called from behind in a weak voice. Vijay was astonished to know that Mr. Raman remembered him. He turned and went back to the bed where the old man expressed his gratitude through his tears.

A couple of days later when Mr. Raman felt recouped enough to converse, Vijay asked the old man,

"Mr. Raman, if I may ask you, why is a man like you, who can earn all luxuries by the virtue of his knowledge and calibre, living a life like this, with no family, no money and not even basic facilities?"

The old man smiled and said not many cared to know the harsh reality of my life. Though they utilized me, none wanted to share my pain. Over time, I have learnt to live with it and now, at this juncture, when my life is at its fag end, I don't care about it. But you have saved my life, I will tell you about myself.

"The initial years of my life were spent in an orphanage, but then destiny smiled upon me for a brief while. A compassionate couple adopted me but soon as fate had it for me, a misunderstanding brew a storm in their relationship. Once again my family was ruined. That is when my role model, the great national leader, Swami Vivekananda inspired me in spirit. Hence, I decided to move away from my family life and dedicate my life to serve the society and the nation at large."

"But in the course of my career as an university professor and a historian, the politics in my close circles dampened my courage and confidence. That was when, as I had told you before, I destroyed all my work, gave up everything and decided to be at the abode of the Lord, where I met my spiritual master."

"I told you everything about me, but I too want to know something from you. I don't think this was a casual visit, was it? In fact, I realized during our conversation last time, that you were not a businessman as you claimed to be. I couldn't comprehend why you were so curious about the temple, until I saw a blurred picture that resembled you, in one of the local dailies the next day of the temple raid, five years ago."

"I guessed you initiated that conversation with me, because you were trying to obtain any information you could get about the temple and the royal family. But I don't have anything against you; I understand you were just doing your job. But do you confess you lied to me?"

Vijay after making sure the room door was securely closed replied, "Yes Mr. Raman, I confess, and my greatest of apologies to you as I hid my true identity to you. But it is the requirement of my profession. But the respect I have for you, sir, is from the bottom of my heart. I truly appreciate your knowledge about the temple and its history. That is why I came seeking your help even this time. Luckily, I was in time and could be of some help to you. I hope you forgive me and help me decode what could be one of the greatest secrets of Indian history."

Mr. Raman was a very broad-minded individual and was always ready to render his services to the nation. He assured Vijay that he completely understood why Vijay hid his true identity. He also said that he would consider himself honoured and blessed by Lord Padmanabha to be useful in rendering any service to the nation.

"Tell me son, how can I help you?"

Vijay took his mobile out, browsed through his gallery of

pictures and showed Mr. Raman the picture he had taken of the engraving on the copper plate and pot found in the vault.

"Can you understand anything from this photograph, Mr. Raman?"

The old man read the engraving in the picture, thought for a while, and then said, "I know about both the kings mentioned in the letter. Karthika Thirunal Rama Varma was known as a true follower of Dharma and he earned the epithet of 'Dharma Raja' because of this. He was generous and kind and is known to have provided asylum to a lot of Christians and Hindus who were fleeing from the religious tyranny of Tipu Sultan. Udit Narayan Singh Sahib Bahadur was the eldest son of Mahip Narayan Singh, who was sadly an incapable administrator and had lost control of his dominions to the English. The son had regular confrontations with the British and, in 1828, petitioned for a re-installation of control to his dominions. May be that is why this letter was sent to Travancore, along with the parcel."

Mr. Raman continued, "In my initial days in Trivandrum, I remember a few disciples of my spiritual guru, who shared common interest in history like me, often spoke about something of great value that was in the royal family's possession. Intrigued by their conversation, my curiosity made me do more research and spoke to the locals who shared legends with me. Rama Varma sent search parties to look for one legendary astrologer Shankar Narayan Namboodiri across Travancore."

"He was finally found in the small village of Manalikkara (part of current Kanyakumari), where he served as a priest at a Sree Krishnaswamy temple. The priest was invited to the palace with due respect. Rama Varma, a noble king, was aware of the ways a scholarly and polished man like the priest had to be treated. The king saluted the priest with great respect by bowing at his feet. Then he washed the priest's feet and sprinkled the water on his head. After being blessed by the priest, the king addressed him, "O great sage! I feel blessed that you accepted my humble invite and set foot in my palace. O great one, please accept my apologies for my ignorance of not being aware of the presence of this knowledge tree in my kingdom. The King of Banaras has sung your glory in his letter to me. How does he know about your prowess?"

The priest smiled pleasantly, blessed the king and replied, "In my teens, when I just tasted the nectar of the Vedas, I happened to meet Shree Vishnu Bharadwaj, who became my master, during his visit to Travancore. He had come to pay his salutation to the Master of the Universe, the Lord Padmanabha. I should thank my stars, because on that fine day, the great man visited the Krishnaswamy temple, where my father was then the priest."

"My father expressed his desire to make me learn the Vedas under Vishnu Bharadwaj. My guru very humbly obliged to take me as his disciple. He took me with him Banaras and after many years of study and practise, I learnt a drop in the ocean of Vedic knowledge, astrology, and little about kaalgnanam (knowledge of time), which also led me to read minds of people."

Once, a group of foreign traders visited the palace making an excuse of doing trade with the king. My guru warned the king against the ill intentions they had of overpowering him in the future. He was able to do this because of his ability to read minds, his knowledge of kaalgnanam, and the power to make prophesies."

Mr. Raman continued, "Years later when King Udit Narayan Singh Sahib Bahadur asked Vishnu Bharadwaj, who served as the king's chief advisor, if he has any worthy disciple who had the calibre to safeguard the secret his ancestors had protected for centuries, Vishnu Bharadwaj pleasantly smiled and nodded in affirmation. But he told the king that the person he had in mind was from a kingdom in southern peninsula.

"The king wished to be introduced to the prodigy, who his chief advisor held in such great esteem and thought had the capability to secure what could be the secret of centuries to come. He did not mind even though he was from a different kingdom."

"That was when young Shankar Narayan Namboodiri was invited to the palace of Banaras. Even at that young age, he had an aura about himself. His body language and his walk were full of confidence and yet, he was humble. He, with great humility, folded his hands in front of the king and saluted him. Shankar Narayan then told the king that he was honoured to be invited to the court. Shankar then asked how could he serve the king?"

"Vishnu Bharadwaj now spoke. He said that the king wanted to know if I had a disciple who was worthy enough whom I could call him my Arjuna? Who could prove my worth as a guru? That is why I have summoned you; I hope you will not let me down, son."

"Oh great sage, it is a given that you are a great guru and there is no need to prove it. Even the king knows it. The question could be if I am a disciple worthy of learning under your able guidance. I will try my best not to let you down, my master. Tell me how could I do that?"

The king began, "You are right. Your guru needs to prove nothing; neither do you. My curiosity to learn about your calibre goes beyond just testing you. If the great sage Vishnu Bharadwaj recommends you, no further testimony is required."

"Now regarding the reason I wanted to see you was the treasure box that will be brought in here in a few minutes. I want you to tell me the worth of what it holds, without opening it."

"Shankar Narayan said with folded hands, "I would try my

best to resolve your apprehensions, your majesty, and bring pride to my guru. The king summoned his men to bring the metal box in question from the treasury. Shankar Narayan fell at Vishnu Bharadwaj's feet seeking his blessings."

"Soon the king's men arrived with a metal box and placed it in front of Shankar. Shankar folded his hands, closed his eyes, and began chanting a mantra. After a couple of minutes he began by saying,

"O great king, from what I have been able to learn in my limited capacity from my great guru, I can see that what this metal box holds in it is worth more than all the gold in this universe. It contains supernatural powers. If used righteously, it can change someone's life for the better. But, on the other hand, if it is used for one's selfish reasons, its powers can destroy the world."

"The king and all of his court stood up astonished, the king himself walked up to Shankar Narayan folded his hands in salute and said, "You are indeed right. This thing in this box is of immeasurable value. I feel blessed to stand amongst the two finest minds of this century—you and your guru. O great one, you are an honour to your parents and to your guru. Your name will be remembered forever in the future as a great legend."

"But how did you do this?"

"Shankar Narayan said, "I read your mind, your majesty. I could read about the thing in the box on your forehead, as you were thinking about it, the moment I looked at the box."

"Vishnu Bharadwaj was very proud of his disciple. He blessed and hugged him. He also told the king very proudly that Shankar had gone ahead of him too. He was capable of even Parakaya Pravesham (astral travelling)."

"The king now ordered all of his court to leave, allowing only his prime minister, the great sage and chief advisor, Vishnu

Bharadwaj, and his disciple Shankar Narayan Namboodiri to remain there."

Mr. Raman after a deep and disappointed sigh said, "I believe the King of Banaras revealed the secret in the box. Now I realize based on this engraved letter, that the secret could be definitely related to the pot you have shown me in the picture. Unfortunately, this is where my research ended; I don't know anything about the pot."

Vijay looked at Mr. Raman puzzled. He wasn't convinced if such things that the old man spoke about existed. He questioned, "Mr. Raman, you really think such things are possible? Do such mystic things happen? We all know how conmen play a few mind games and fool innocent people."

"We have reached Mars, we have invented atomic weapons,but still, scientists and physicists are struggling to decipher the mysteries time holds in it."

"You are telling me ancient sages, who didn't know anything but few ancient scriptures, could do stuff like astral travelling, read minds with pinpoint accuracy? You want me to believe this, Mr. Raman?"

Mr. Raman took a deep breath, and spoke again, "What do you mean a few ancient scriptures? In Sanskrit, 'Veda' means knowledge. The Vedic civilization was at a much higher level of development than our modern society. From the standpoint of current evolutionary theory, the human race is supposed to be at the top of the social development. However, according to the Vedic literature, in the distant past, there have been many civilizations in the world, the greatness of which we cannot even imagine.

The Vedas, the Indian epics and Puranic texts were studied in detail in Mumbai in 1975. The knowledge gained during this study was quite explosive—believed many physicists and scientists then. The Bhagvat Purana, believed to be written over 5000 years ago, describes atoms as paramanuh, the final material manifestation. Everything around us are created, when many such atoms combine. The Bhagvat Purana also describes time scales.

Relativity theory and nuclear physics are subjects mentioned in many Sanskrit texts. The Aryans seemed to be aware of electricity, nuclear weapons and even superconductivity. The effect of a nuclear weapon is described in the Mahabharatha as follows—the heat from this weapon seemed to create a fever across the earth. The sun seemed to have come down to earth in the form of concentric circles. It was as if nature's fury was unleashed with abandon.

While we know of aeroplanes being invented by the Wright Brothers in 1903, Shivkar Talpade is believed to have built a flying machine that ran on solar energy and mercury. Although the subject is mired in controversy, he seems to have built this machine using data from Vedic texts.

However, flying saucers do find a mention in Ramayana. They were referred to as vimanas, which belonged to King Ravana of Lanka. The vimana is described as having walls glittering with encrusted diamonds and golden windows. This could fly anywhere under the command of a pilot or it could even hover one place in mid-air.

The Vedas also talk about different skills and techniques such as Ashwadridaya and Akshhridaya. The former was the skill to talk to and control horses and the latter was the incredible skill of counting the number of fruits and leaves in any tree in an instant.

"Whatever you narrated sir is legendary and is mythical. It is difficult to believe and doesn't have any concrete proof to be accepted as truth. Can you speak about anything in that occurred in today's world?", asked Vijay.

Mr. Raman replied, "Yes. Let me tell you about the shining star of philosophers,Adi Sankara or Sankara Bhagvatpada, who is an undisputed Advaitin. His commentaries and explanations of various Upanishads, Brahma Sutras, and other Vedic texts stand tall even today. He is given the credit of reinstalling Hinduism to its earlier popularity and fame, although this journey was fraught with problems and difficulties. His story comes to us through a text called Madhaviya Sankara Digvijaya, which is taken by most scholars as the final authority on Adi Sankara's life.

Adi Sankara realized that the only way the old Vedic system can be recovered and the many sects unified together was to debate and win against pundits who followed various the ritualistic forms of Hinduism. His biggest challenge was against Mandana Mishra, a big scholar of his time who had his tutelage under the powerful guru, Kumarila Bhatta.

Mandana Mishra and Udaya Bharti formed an ideal couple of those times. She was also well versed in all the texts and books. After a heated debated, Adi Sankara was on the verge on winning against Mandana Mishra who was ready to accept defeat. However, his wife stopped him and questioned Adi Sankara, "How can you, a sanyasi, say you know everything there is to know about our texts? You have not lived the life of a householder or of an ordinary citizen. Debate and win against me on those topics and then, we can accept my defeat." Thus saying, she started expounded on laws and obligations of marriage and related householder issues to which Adi Sankara could not respond appropriately. Udaya Bharti agreed to give him some time to learn and master these texts and return to complete the debate.

Adi Sankara agreed and using his yogic powers was able to enter the body of a king who had just died. Before that, he gave instructions to his disciples to preserve his body. The king whose body the soul of Adi Sankara entered was earlier an evil, cruel king and yet, loved by his wives.

When suddenly, the king seemed to wake up from his death, the wives were surprised but happy as well. Adi Sankara lived the life of a king, householder, and husband learnt everything about those shastras as well. When it was time to return to his original body, he blessed the woman who taught him all this.

When he returned to the debate, he easily won over Udaya Bharti and she became an ardent follower of Adi Sankara and Advaita philosophy.

Vijay was very impressed by Mr. Raman's knowledge, but was not completely convinced about his argument. Hence, he questioned again, "Mr. Raman, you are a learned man. I am quite sure you wouldn't have believed all this without seeing it for yourself. Please tell me what made you believe?"

Mr. Raman replied, "Yes I will tell you about my own experience and here there is no ambiguity or exaggeration. You remember I told you about my spiritual master and a few of his disciples who often spoke about the great possession of the royal family of Travancore?"

"The first time I went to his ashram (abode), I was a stranger in Trivandrum. Not only that, as I told you before, I myself was stranger to my past, my childhood. As soon as my spiritual guru looked at me, he said I claimed to be someone I was not. Naturally, I had no clue about what he was saying. Then he explained that he was talking about my surname. How did a man who had never seen me know I was adopted from an orphanage?"

"Since then whatever he has predicted for me has come true, and I began believing him. He had also told me that my name would be part of history. I did not understand his statement. But after today's conversation with you, it seems to me that you are going to make history and I am going to be part of it."

Mr. Raman suddenly began to choke. He had an asthma attack. Maybe talking for a long time continuously and the excitement with which he did it was the cause for it. Vijay immediately rushed to get the doctor to attend to the old man. After a few hours when Mr. Raman was able to talk, he sent for Vijay, as he wanted to tell him something that could help his case.

Mr. Raman called Vijay close and in a week voice said, "King of Travancore, Karthika Thirunal Rama Varma, requested Shankar Narayan to be the chief priest at the Padmanabha Temple, to which he gladly agreed. Since the day he accepted this responsibility, his lineage has continued to be the chief priest of the temple. This continued till almost couple of decades ago."

Vijay immediately asked frowning in thought, "What happened two decades ago?"

Mr. Raman replied, "If you remember our conversation five years ago, I had told you the last person of Shankar's lineage who became the chief priest died in a fire accident and his grandson went missing."

Vijay trying to cover the anxiety in his voice asked the old man, "Are you saying that the chief priest who died almost two decades ago was of Shankar Narayan's lineage?"

Mr. Raman replied, "Yes."

That one word stabbed Vijay like a cold knife in the heart. The thoughts of his ancestors being involved in covering up a secret of such magnitude clouded his mind. He didn't know whether any of his ancestors, except Shankar Narayan, knew about the secret of the pot. He wondered if it was in the national interest or mankind at large, or did they have any selfish motives?

Did his grandfather knew about the pot? In that case, was his death related to the secret he was guarding? Was his credibility, his sincerity as an investigating officer at stake? His experience in holding his nerve in such pressurised situations helped him to make sure that he didn't express his emotions to Mr. Raman. His ethical values, commitment and sincerity towards his job made him concerned about the secret the pot held within. He knew that if the findings he had made till now about the pot, were even close to being true, then the pot would be a national treasure and its security a matter of high priority.

He also knew that even if he fails to decipher the secret of the pot, it had to be protected along with the enormous riches in the vaults of the temple. If those riches fall in wrong hands, it could bring grave danger to humanity at large. He realized he had to make sure the top officials paid attention to securing the temple efficiently.

Though the security had been tightened to a great extent after the temple vaults were opened in 2011 Vijay felt better security arrangement was needed. He felt that mere deployment of armed police officers and round-the-clock mobile police patrolling was not enough and that hi-tech devices were also needed to protect the riches of the temple.

Looking at Mr. Raman's condition, Vijay felt he was stable and hence, he felt it was time for him to get back to work. He wished the old man well, promised him that if he succeeds in decoding the secret of the pot and if there was an opportunity to reveal it to the world, Mr. Raman would get the credit due to him. He reached the government guest house, where Akshay was almost done with the report regarding the findings of the temple.

Vijay reviewed the report and noticed that recommendations to tighten the security were limited to increasing the strength of armed police men around the temple. He attributed this error to the lack of experience and amateurishness on his junior's part. That is when Vijay asked, "Do you know about the bank robbery that happened a couple of years ago in Haryana's Gohana town?"

Akshay looked at him with a confused expression but then after a brief moment he had realized his mistake. Vijay continued a Hollywood-style bank heist was carried out by a gang of robbers at Punjab National Bank. Jewelery and cash, worth crores of rupees, were stolen. The robbers dug a tunnel 2.5 feet in width and 125 feet in length from an old abandoned building across the street to the strong room of the bank."

"Police officers were seen inspecting the tunnel, which seems to have escaped the notice until the robbers had long gone.

The building was covered with the dirt obtained during the digging process. Windows were barred to dull the noise created by the digging activity. About 90 lockers were surely being broken open and it's contents lost. The gang must have been working for more than a month to complete the tunnel."

In another similar bank heist in Kerala, a hole was dug through the floor of a bank to its strong room. Cash and about 80 kilograms of gold were stolen. In this case, the police did manage to catch the culprits and the gang leader confessed that he was inspired by an idea shown in a popular Bollywood film.

"When a few crores can make people do outrageous things like this, imagine what a treasure worth billions of dollars like the one you saw in the temple do? Gangs of thugs around the world could be after this treasure and with technological advancements around the world, like deep bore used in subway construction. Boring machines are inserted into a hole dug at a convenient spot along the proposed line, and then proceeded through the earth little by little—more than eighty feet per day—until they have carved out space along the entire corridor."

"These boring machines are powerful and can be very unobtrusive to the common man as the entire activity would be carried down under the earth allowing for greater flexibility to the workers and designers.

In fact, you would not even know a subway was being built.

These machines are capable of drilling holes as wide as 50 feet. I will not be surprised if some sophisticated group of criminals does attempt to loot the temple and no one gets a clue just as these bank burglars did their job without any disruption. Hence, we, as the top security agency of this nation, have to be prepared for everything."

Vijay advised Akshay to amend the report and also in turn to be prepared for everything in life. But he himself was not still prepared to accept the possibility of his ancestors being involved in all of this. His mind was still in turbulence. Suddenly, he asked himself, "Was it sheer coincidence that I have heard my grandfather's voice in my dreams or was it that my grandfather's spirits trying to convey something to me after all these years?

Something told him it was end of the road for him in Trivandrum. But he had no clue where he had to go from there or what he had to do for the next piece of information. But he knew for a fact that he would find it extremely difficult to continue his investigation officially.

What kept him from declaring his findings immediately was he had no solid evidence of the prowess of the pot, except the copper engravings and the story that Mr. Raman had spoken of. The story may not even be true. He had no idea about the veracity of it. But Vijay had made up his mind about declaring his biological connection with Shankar Narayan, if he found solid reason for doing so. He didn't care if it puts his name in controversy.

He decided to request for a long leave, while submitting the report of the temple raid, in Delhi to his superiors in a few days. But before heading back to Delhi, he knew he had to visit his father in Bangalore.

A few days later, Vijay was summoned by the director of IB. He had gone through every word of the report faxed to him by Vijay. He began,

"I have gone through your report on the findings of the Sree Padmanabha Swamy Temple. Congratulations on successfully completing yet another mission under your able leadership. I specially appreciate the security recommendations you have made. I will make sure that the home ministry pays attention to the recommendations on the security arrangements at the temple that you and your team have mentioned."

"Along with the report, I also had a look at your application for leave and I have approved it too. On a personal front, I want to know, was this assignment so taxing that you have applied for a three-week leave? I don't remember you applying for leave even when you came back from a cross-border mission successfully accomplishing it after 26/11 attack—when you looked into the eyes of death itself, and returned alive. I didn't see a wrinkle of fear on your face at that moment. Did this simple raid on a temple tire you down so much that you are availing leave?"

Vijay replied I need a break, sir."

"As far as I have known you son, I can say one thing without a doubt. You aren't a guy who can enjoy a break from work. You are not only the best of the agents I have, you are also Vikramaditya's son. He was my best friend since the days of my training. Hence, you are like my family. If something is troubling you, you can always come and talk to me."

The director continued in a candid way this time or have you found something in the temple that you want to investigate unofficially? Anyway, on a serious note, you know the protocol. You need to report to duty wherever you are if duty calls you."

Saying this he laughed out loud. Vijay too joined him with a tight lipped smile.

CHAPTER 5

Hours later, lying on his couch, Vijay was wondering what he should do next? Suddenly, like a flash of lightning, an idea struck him. He shouted, "Banaras University!" But how will he go there as an IB officer? People there will definitely feel conscious and may not cooperate in the investigation. He realized he had to use a disguise. But who does he disguise himself as, was the question. At that very moment, he remembered the person in the University who could help him.

It was the principal of the University, who was Vijay's college professor and an ex-service man at IMA. Vijay reached out to his mobile and sent out a text, which read Emergency, have to meet."

A reply came in no time. The message read, "Tomorrow, 11 a.m., my office."

The next day Vijay waited at the principal's office at the Delhi University, thirty minutes ahead of schedule. That is how the professor liked his meetings to begin. People who came to meet him had to arrive at least twenty minutes prior to the meeting and was expected to be meticulously prepared for it, which included the attire.

It had been quite a few years since Vijay had met the professor, but he was sure enough nothing would have changed the attitude of the man. Vijay still vividly remembered the professor's stern attitude with which he lived his life too. For him, life was a codebook of army rules and discipline. He lived by the book and died by the book.

He himself saw his role as to reinstate order and organization into the IMA. He was a strong-willed, opinionated and a combative man. For him, discipline had become his second skin. It has reached to such an extent that his leadership had transformed a civil university of Delhi into a pseudo-military academy. Vijay patiently sat in the reception, waiting for the professor to call him in. He wondered if his formal dress code was precise, as the professor liked it.

Was the colour combination he was wearing matched the colour of his shoes? Were the clothes perfectly ironed? Vijay's mind ran halter-skelter to make sure he hadn't missed anything that could catch the eye of the professor. He knew if the professor lost his temper once, getting his attention again was nearly impossible.

The moment the gong struck twenty minutes to 11, the phone on the receptionist's desk sprang to life. A deep voice within the phone instructed the receptionist to allow the gentleman in, who was waiting in the lobby. Vijay knocked on the door and was summoned in by the voice.

The old professor was an absolute lookalike of Sean Connery, who is best known for portraying the legendary character of the British spy, James Bond. The man's cautious, prudent and rather self-contained eyes were what set him apart from the crowd. He always had a very realistic approach towards life and never was inclined to take foolish chances or be carried away by the overly optimistic or idealistic schemes of starry-eyed dreamers. That is what made him one of Vijay's role models.

Both the men formally shook hands and Vijay was asked to have a seat. Both men exchanged a handshake—the warmth of which said a lot about the high regard they had for each other.

"Welcome Vijay, it's been a long time since we met. But I have read and heard a lot about your achievements through the media. It makes me proud that you were one of the students I trained."

"Thank you Sir. I also extend my gratitude for this appointment on such short notice, Sir. This was really important and I really appreciate your response."

The professor nodded and smiled and then without wasting a moment, the old disciplinarian got to the point. He began, "Tell me officer, what is it that made you visit me in such a hurry?"

Vijay took a moment to respond, and then said Sir, I am on a national security mission and to accomplish the same, I need to stay in Banaras under cover for a while. For which, I need to disguise myself as a research scholar. I need your help regarding the credentials to prove my status as a research scholar."

"In that case, why didn't this request come as an official one?"

"Because this isn't an official mission sir, I am asking this as a personal favour."

"And what makes you think, I will be ready to do this for you?"

"Sir, I agree I have no official permission to carry out this mission. But the reason for me to begin this investigation is national security. Though I am going out of my way to accomplish this mission in a personal capacity, it is rooted in the vision of doing larger good to the country. I am sure if we don't pay attention to this concern, we will be welcoming grave danger to our nation, and mankind, at large."

"In that case, why didn't you choose to bring your concerns to official notice?"

"Sir, according to my speculations, the secret I hold could prove to be one of the greatest secrets of our country and the most dangerous as well. My experience as a spy has taught me enough to understand that even walls have ears and such secrets have to be guarded even at the risk of losing one's life. At least, until you gather enough safe keepers and the system is ready to guard it. Hence, I cannot make my investigation official as yet sir. I hope you understand my point of view."

Though the professor was stuck by the rulebook, he made an exception to it. The situation that brought this exception to life, very rarely though, was concern to national security or national wealth. The intensity and the conviction Vijay had in his eyes while he was talking, forced the professor to believe him.

The professor was aware of Vijay's capabilities since his training days, and also knew that he wouldn't raise a concern of the kind he has right now unless he felt very strongly about it. Hence, he said Alright, I will arrange for what you have asked for officer. But make sure you use it well. I don't want the university's name to get involved in unnecessary controversies. I am sure you know what you are doing."

Vijay nodded in affirmation and rose to leave. He extended his hand to thank the man and take his leave. Just before Vijay stepped out, the professor wished him luck, which surprised Vijay. The professor was a person who very rarely expressed his feelings. Vijay accepted his wishes but was a little confused about what made one of the emotionally strongest men he had known feel a little tensed.

Was it the severity of the situation, or was it the concern he had for his favourite officer? Was the professor concerned about Vijay's safety as he could be for anybody else? Vijay pushed all the thoughts out of his mind, considered the professor's best wishes as a good omen and left his office.

The next day, Vijay had a letter and the required documents to prove he was a research scholar. These documents were delivered to his residence from the Delhi University. He, by then, had booked a train ticket to Banaras in the new super fast express from Delhi for the same evening. He kept the letter from the University safely in his luggage and before leaving for to the railway station, he called his father for his blessing. But he couldn't, as the doctor told him his father was suffering from great pain.

When Vijay asked if he should postpone his travel, Major Vikramaditya screamed saying, "Your responsibility of who you are must be of highest priority. Consider me dead if your come to see me without finishing what you started. Don't even call me unless you want to tell me you accomplished your mission. I fight my battles—you fight yours."

Though Vijay had to go with a heavy heart, he knew it was his father's attempt to push him not to quit his responsibility as a soldier on his mission. Vijay had no clue what to expect during his stay at Banaras. But he knew a heck of a journey was about to begin. He hoped he would meet someone in the train who could know something that could be useful to him, which is a rare possibility in a plane.

Vijay didn't happen to meet anyone he was hoping for. But he did meet a couple of people in the train who catalysed his determination to solve the mystery of the pot. It had been just couple of hours since the journey had begun. Two young men, who seemed to have lived overseas for some years, got into the train at the Agra station.

The two men, like any other person who had lived in a developed foreign country, were complaining and comparing the infrastructure of the West to that in India. It was not at all surprising to hear them complain. They concluded that the problems in this country are the result of corruption.

Vijay too agreed with that point; but something they went on to say triggered his emotions. He was never a person who picked an argument usually unnecessarily. But when they ridiculed the nation by saying every soul in this country has become corrupt, he felt anger rising in him. A few years ago,people believed that the only department sincerely doing their job is the defence force. But even that turned out to be an illusion. This country has no future.

Vijay couldn't control himself any longer. He began, "Excuse me! I know I don't have a right to intervene in your discussion. But being a true citizen of this country, I will not stay mum when anyone ridicules my motherland. You better listen to what I have to say."

The two men were stunned to see a stranger react to their conversation regarding the nation. They believed that no one cared a damn of what people thought about their own country. But the man talking to them was different. The intensity with which Vijay charged them forced them to listen to him.

Vijay continued, "I also agree that this country, which we call our motherland, has some problems. But which country in this world is perfect? Every country has its own set of problems. It is also up to the country's citizens to contribute and involve in the process of solving the nation's issues. But people like you, who spend their early life here to study, equip themselves to face life challenges here. But then you go on to serve in foreign lands without caring about out motherland. If you have a problem with the situation here, why didn't you try changing it?"

"How could we, with such a corrupt system in place?"

"By being a part of the system—by being in position of IPS and IAS officers—by being a part of the national politics—by being the change you want to see around you. I agree with what you said. Even the defence forces are a part of this very system.

But because of a few corrupt people, you don't call the entire Indian defence corrupt and coward."

"You might be wondering why I am talking so much. I might not even have any personal experience. But that isn't true. I will tell you my father's experience, who is an Ashoka Chakra awardee. If you aren't aware of the Ashoka Chakra, then let me explain to you what it means. The Ashoka Chakra is India's highest peacetime military decoration award that is awarded for valour, courageous action or self-sacrifice. It is equivalent to the peacetime, the Param Vir Chakra, and is awarded for the most conspicuous bravery or some daring or pre-eminent valour or self-sacrifice other than in the face of the enemy."

"My father, Major Vikramaditya was a well-known theatre artist, who proved his mettle at the national level drama competition that was held in Lucknow. A few RAW officials, who had come to witness the event, noticed his acting prowess."

Thinking that his skills could be of use to the country, RAW offered him a contract to pose as an undercover agent in Pakistan, to which my father readily agreed. He was trained under RAW, changed his identity completed, and went to Pakistan as Ahmed Khan at the age of 23. During his two-year rigorous training period with RAW in Delhi, he was trained in religious education, he learnt Punjabi and Urdu—languages that were spoken widely all across Pakistan—and even under circumcision surgery to pass off as a staunch Muslim.

At Pakistan, in the guise of Ahmed Khan, he did his LLB for 3 years at Karachi University, and joined the Pakistan army, where he was soon promoted to the level of a Major. He passed on a lot of critical information to India during his entire stay in Pakistan, which proved very useful to India.

Major Vikramaditya's cover was blown during one of the telegraphic exchanges. He was captured, tortured, and sentenced to life imprisonment at the Karachi jail."

By now, the two men were extremely intrigued by listening to Vijay's narration. They were listening to Vijay as if it was an edge of the seat thriller.

"Is he still in some jail across the border? Didn't the Indian agencies do anything to get him back to India, as is the case with most countries, when all communications are cut off, if their spy is caught on a mission in foreign land?"

"True. Most countries do this and India is no different. But my father was too smart to stay captured and waiting for help to arrive."

The two men asked eagerly, "Please tell us how did he manage to escape?"

"He convinced 7-8 men who were charged of petty crimes and serving their sentences at Sialkot to jailbreak with him. These men, along with my father, sawed off the iron rod of the ward in which they were stationed, to create an escapable gap of nearly one feet. They managed to jailbreak with two supportive factors. Firstly, due to the number of prisoners in one cell. Secondly, because of the slew of grease."

"The toothed edge of iron filer was dipped in grease to mute the sawing operation. After couple of minutes, the tongue-less filer did everything with its tooth and allowed prisoners the to beat their way out of the cell. After coming out from the jail bars, they scaled the eight feet high inner boundary and the fourteen feet high outer wall, by making a human ladder. They also made a rope using towel, dhoti and shawl to pull out all escapees. He also managed to inform Indian agencies about his escape through the sea as escaping through land could be more dangerous. But he didn't have time to send the exact co-ordinates where they could send help to bring him back to safety."

"He risked his life and managed to reach the Karachi port, where he managed to steal a local fishing boat. He rowed it for almost 20 hours continuously and reached a village at the Pakistani border and entered India through the Gulf of Kutch."

"He was then given complete care at the army hospital, but the torture he underwent at Karachi had infected his leg. It had to be amputated to avoid further infection. He had to retire from active services since then."

"Sir, weren't you inspired to join after your father retired?"

"I was. My father too was of the same opinion. But, as I was the only son, the other members of my extended family convinced my father against it. Now I am a historian and I am serving the nation in my own capacity."

"Thank you, sir, for making us realize the intensity of the situation. We never had this perception about our nation. After graduating from college we were dazzled by the glamour and wealth of the West that sent us on a wild goose chase. But now we understand our share of responsibilities towards our nation."

"That was exactly my intention. I am sorry if I have hurt your feelings in any way. Our country can reach the zenith of progress, if all of us realize our responsibilities and act accordingly. I wish you boys best wishes for your future."

"Thank you sir."

All the three rested for a few hours through the night after this lengthy conversation and when they woke up the next day, they had reached the holy city of Banaras. The train reached the destination exactly at 5:10 a.m. It was still dark. Vijay hired a rickshaw and asked him to take him to a hotel near Banaras Hindu University, where he could refresh and get ready to visit the University.

On the way to the hotel, the rickshaw passed the famous Vishwanath temple. The rickshaw driver, an old but talkative person, casually asked, "Sir you missed the early morning *mangala aarti* (part of the Hindu religious ritual of worship, in which light from wicks soaked in *ghee* (purified butter) or camphor is offered to one or more deities). It happens between 3 a.m. to 4 a.m. The *mangala aarti* performed is worth watching and it is pious to perform *puja* after that. While Srinagar (deity decoration) is going on, devotional songs that are played, will take you to different world."

Vijay was not paying attention to the driver. He was thinking whether his professor's recommendation letter will be sufficient to convince the principal of BHU. But the driver went on talking merrily.

"Sir, you can still bathe in the holy Ganges. A bath in the river Ganges is one of many methods believed to lead one on a path to *Moksha* (liberation). Thus, Hindus from all over the world try to visit the place at least once in their lifetime. Then you can have a *darshan* (sacred sight) of early morning decoration of lord Vishwanath.

Pointing to the two domes of the temple, the driver said The two domes of the temple are covered by gold, donated by Maharaja Ranjit Singh."

Vijay still hadn't spoken a word. He wasn't even listening to the driver. He abruptly asked, "How far is the hotel?"

The rickshaw driver then realised that his passenger may not be interested in what he was saying all this while. He also had a hunch that the passenger may be struggling to find the true sense of belief. But he was not sure if his passenger would take his advice in the right sense.

He earnestly replied, "We are almost there sir."

"And how far is the University campus from the hotel?"

"Not much sir—just 2 k.m. It could be 10 minutes by a rickshaw and may be a maximum of 20 minutes if you choose to walk."

The rickshaw stopped in a few minutes, at a board that read 'Hotel Vishwanath'. Vijay stepped down from the rickshaw, checked the meter and paid the driver. He picked his luggage turned and was about to get into the hotel. The driver by then had mustered enough courage to speak out. He said,

"Sir, I know this is none of my business. But I hope you would respect my age and listen to what I want to say."

Vijay was surprised to see the driver's behaviour. But he didn't want to be rude to the old man. He very politely said, "Please tell me, sir."

"I have seen a lot of life and my experience with life tells me, you aren't at peace from within. I also feel you are not a believer in the Almighty, though I don't know the reason for this. But if a true devotee prays to lord Shiva with a pure heart, the Lord grants all his wishes and relieves him from all his worldly sorrows; even from death and the cycle of rebirth. I am sure the Lord will show his mercy on you too, you just have to seek for it."

Vijay smiled at the rickshaw driver and entered the hotel. The driver prayed in his mind to Lord Shiva to be merciful on Vijay and went on his way.

Vijay rested for a while in his hotel room and then got ready to visit the principal of BHU. As he had decided to disguise himself as a historian and research scholar, who wanted to pursue research the royal family of Banaras, he wore a kurta pyjama (Indian ethnic wear). He also made sure he carried the recommendation letter that would prove to be his permission letter to begin his investigation.

At around 10 a.m., he entered the campus and was on his way to the principal's office. He passed the huge statue of Bharat Ratna, Pandit Madan Mohan Malviya, who founded BHU in 1916. While he was looking for a way to reach the principal's office, he fortunately found few students of the University.

They showed him the way and helped him reach the principal's office, where he saw an office boy lazing on a wooden stool outside the principal's office. Vijay went and requested him to give the recommendation letter he had brought. After five minutes the office boy came back and asked Vijay to go in and meet the principal. He stood at the door step and asked, "May I come in, sir?"

The BHU principal looked up and said, "Please do."

He extended his hand and shook Vijay's hand. He was surprised at the firmness of the handshake. He wondered, "Can just a research scholar possess such a firm handshake? The youth these days is taking their fitness very seriously."

"Please have a seat."

Both men sat and then the principal began I read the letter you brought Vijay; I hope you don't mind me calling you by your name."

Vijay nodded in affirmation.

"I will be more than happy to admit you as a research scholar at BHU. Your professor is a tough taskmaster, I know him since his young days. If he has such a high regard for you, I don't need further proof of your capabilities. I assure you of all the assistance you need for your research here. I will get all the formalities for your admission and stay in our hostel complete by today."

"But I will ask the hostel warden to let you settle down in one of the rooms. You just submit a photo and few other documents in the admin department."

Also you tell me a little about your research, so that I can get you appropriate help."

Vijay replied, "Thank you sir for your concern. Regarding my research, I am a historian, sir. I want to pursue my research about the most famous royal families of India and the royal family of Banaras is one of them. If you can introduce me to someone who can help me in this regard, I will be grateful. Also if you could introduce me to someone well-versed in Sanskrit, it will be very helpful."

"Don't worry, the faculty I am going to introduce you to, fulfils both of your requirements. He is one of the most credible and knowledgeable faculties we have in our University. He has a doctorate in Sanskrit. I will introduce you to him tomorrow. For now, you can go and settle down in the hostel."

Vijay thanked the principal once again and took his leave. He decided to go back to hotel to get his luggage and settle down in the University hostel. But before that, he wanted to go on a campus tour. He began his tour from the main campus on the banks of the Ganges. He leisurely walked through the campus layout which was approximately a semicircle, with intersecting roads laid out along the radii or in arcs.

He first visited the Sayaji Rao Gaekwad Library, which is the main library on campus. It was a huge library. Students were referring and studying when Vijay entered the library, hence he couldn't talk to anyone including the librarian. But he read a board which declared the treasures of the library. Designated as the Manuscript Conservation Centre (MCC), which falls under the National Mission for Manuscripts that was set up in 2003, this humongous library has over 1.3 million books.

Then he went to Bharat Kala Bhavan, an art and archaeological museum, displaying a big collection of Indian paintings, archaeological artefacts, costumes and other textiles, philately along with archival, and literary materials.

By the time he exited the museum, it was late afternoon. Vijay thought that it was time he must go back to the hotel, have some lunch, and get his luggage to settle down in the hostel. On his way to the hotel, he passed the Indian Institute of Technology (IIT), India's premier engineering institutes and Sir Sunderlal Hospital, a teaching hospital for the Institute of Medical Sciences.

By the time Vijay returned from the hotel with his luggage, the University admin department had completed all the formalities regarding Vijay's admission. The next day Vijay visited the principal again and requested him for an introduction to the Sanskrit faculty he was talking about the previous day. The principal immediately obliged and called for the faculty.

Ten minutes later, a middle-aged man dressed in dhoti and kurta (a traditional garment worn by male Hindus) entered the room. He wore a tilak on his forehead and maintained a sikha hairstyle (a lock of hair, left on top or on the back of the shaved head of a male Orthodox Hindu. Though traditionally all Hindus were required to wear a sikha, today it is seen mainly among Brahmins and temple priests.)

As the faculty reached the doorstep he asked, "May I come in sir?"

The principal responded, "Please do, Dr. Joshi."

As Vijay stood up facing Dr. Joshi, the principal began the introductions.

"Vijay, this is Dr. Joshi. He is a scholar of ancient history and has also published various journals on World History. His book on Indian history, Medieval India, shows his substantial knowledge about India and its royal families. He also is an eminent Sanskrit scholar. If there is something he can't read, translate or explain in Sanskrit, I doubt anyone else can in this country. I am sure he will be of great help to you in your research on royal families of India as he belongs to one of the oldest families in the town and knows everything worth knowing about Banaras."

Vijay extended his arm to shake Dr. Joshi's hand, but the doctor folded his hands in a traditional Namaste. Vijay smiled and returned the Namaste. The principal now was about to introduce Vijay. But before he could, Dr. Joshi said, "I have seen you somewhere, but I can't remember where!"

Vijay wondered if the professor was referring to seeing his photo in the media, when he was awarded the Kirti Chakra. Hoping he was wrong, he tried to divert his attention.

"Remember seeing me sir? Yes, could be possible! A couple of months ago I had written an article in one of the dailies about the youth's take on going to the West, in the quest of their dreams. The article received a lot of attention. It also had my photo, may be that is what you are relating to."

Fortunately, Dr. Joshi didn't dig deep into it and the principal also intervened Dr. Joshi, this is Vijay. He is a bright research scholar from the Delhi University. He is here to continue his research on the royal families of India—the royal family of Banaras being one of the families he wants to research on. I have asked him to seek your help for the same. I request you to oblige him."

"Sure sir. The young man can come to see me whenever he wants. I'll do the needful."

Vijay told Dr. Joshi that he would reach out to him if required, thanked both the men, and left for the hostel. But Dr. Joshi stayed back to request the principal to see Vijay's academic record in his documents,with which the principal was mighty impressed.

That evening wandering and thinking what his next move must be, Vijay just hoped he would get some lead about the pot from Dr. Joshi. Walking along the streets of Banaras, he reached the banks of the Ganges. It was the southern part of the bank area. In ancient times, the river Assi used to flow.

Assi-ghat is part of an official pilgrim road; here he saw pilgrims having a bath in the Ganges before proceeding for the evening darshan of Lord Vishvanath. Vijay sat there and watched yogis meditate with deep concentration, pilgrims lighting sacred lamps and letting them afloat in the river, which was believed to wash away their sins.

As he sat there, the crowd at the bank kept on increasing, Vijay wondered, a walk along the banks of Banaras is a unique experience even for a non-believer like him.

He felt some kind of positive energy and peace fill him from within. Though he couldn't understand the reason, he couldn't also deny the experience. But he still couldn't accept divinity. He wondered looking at all the tens and hundreds of people gathering at the bank of the Ganges.

"What makes all these people believe in something they have never seen and know only what at best could be legendary? Practically they pray to a stone to solve all their problems!"

Staring at the crowd, he was taken back in time to his childhood days, when he used to see people flock to the Anantha Padmanabha Swamy Temple, seeking His blessings. Among His greatest devotees was his grandfather himself, but still had to die a brutal death with none of his kin around him when he breathed his last and that is what turned Vijay to an atheist.

Then he thought of Major Vikramaditya, who although was a noble person but still, was suffering from an incurable pain. These were the reasons why he couldn't redeem his faith.

As he was lost in his memories, a pat on his back brought him back to the present. To Vijay's pleasant surprise, it was Dr. Joshi with his family. He had come to Assi-ghat for the evening *aarti* and for a *darshan* of the Lord. Vijay was thrilled to see him. He hoped to begin a long conversation with him.,While he was thinking how to start the conversation, Dr. Joshi said, "Mr. Vijay, pleasure to see you here. Why don't you join us for the *puja*?"

"No doctor. I am comfortable here, watching the flowing river. You please carry on."

Vijay said this with a smile. Dr. Joshi was not only intrigued by Vijay's response, but also he saw a touch of sarcasm in his smile. He wondered, "Is this young man not at peace with himself and with the lord? If so, what is it that is troubling him?" Something from within him made him feel he had to help Vijay. He asked him to stay till he came back from the temple. Vijay nodded in agreement. But he wondered why the doctor had asked him to stay!

After a while when Dr. Joshi got back with his family, he saw Vijay sitting with his feet immersed in the river. He went to Vijay and invited him home for dinner. He looked at his host puzzled, and asked,

"Dinner invitation for me, sir. But why? You hardly know me! You don't have to bother yourself sir, I will be fine."

"Not at all a bother my friend. Banaras has a custom of treating its guests as gods. Don't you remember the saying, Atithi devo bhava (Guests are gods). My family still believes in this phrase. I request you to join us."

Vijay was overwhelmed by Dr. Joshi's invitation and couldn't decline it. On the way to the host's house, Vijay asked, "Doctor don't you think the concept of godliness was just to instill fear in the heart of people by kings and monarchs back in history? And now fake pundits and astrologers are doing great business out of this fear?"

"You are right my friend. Nowadays, godliness is becoming a money-making method. But that is just one side of the coin— it doesn't mean god doesn't exist. If I may ask you, how the universe did come into existence? Youth like you with the so-called modern outlook will pull out the name of the Big Bang theory, but the Big Bang is not the beginning of everything."

"Steven Weinberg, a Nobel laureate in Physics, said at the moment of this explosion, "the universe was about a hundred thousand million degrees centigrade and the universe was filled with light."

"The universe has not always existed. It had a start point. What caused that? Scientists have no explanation for the sudden explosion of light and matter. But Hindu scriptures like the Vedas and the Puranas clearly explain all aspects of cosmology, evolution, and astronomy."

"Just imagine if the Hindu scriptures can decipher the hidden secrets of the evolution of the universe, what can't it do? It is unfortunate that we Indians are still ignorant of its powers, whereas the world is trying to explore it."

Vijay was listening intently and he added, "Not sure if the Vedas and Puranas are utilized properly, but am sure a lot of Indian talent is serving the West to the best of its ability, but is not serving the motherland."

"You are right Vijay. It surprises me that people from across the world come to the Banaras University to study various subjects, including technology at the IIT. But our own Indian students go abroad to study. What saddens me the most is that they not only study there but also settle down there never to come back."

Vijay felt he had matched the right frequency with Dr. Joshi and this was the opportunity to prolong the conversation and get more information about the royal family of Banaras, its confidants and, if possible, the pot itself. Hence Vijay continued Dr. Joshi, you are not only an authority in history but you also seem to know a lot about Hindu scriptures, astronomy and probably astrology, isn't it?"

"Not a lot my friend, but yes. I can say I know what you can consider a drop in an ocean of Hindu scriptures and astrology. I belong to family of astrologers and whatever little I have learnt, I owe it to my ancestors. Fourteen generations of my family were astrologers for the royal family."

"Fourteen generations of people who believed in astrology! Are you kidding me?"

"No I am not, my friend. They were not just believers, but were ace at predictions. None of their predictions went wrong, not one! They all came true with pinpoint precession.

Vijay was amused by the fact that the man knew his family tree from the beginning. What struck him was a thought that as the man knew about 14 of his preceding generations; he himself might know or would lead Vijay to someone who knows something about the pot. But he couldn't directly get to the topic; hence he continued to listen intently though he wasn't convinced with what he heard,

Dr. Joshi continued But it is not just family sentiment or affection towards my ancestors that makes me want to remember them. It is the Indian culture to know, remember and respect our ancestors. India, besides being known for various accomplishments, is also known for its humility, kindness and hospitality. It is sad that the current crop of youngsters have forgotten this. If they don't know, appreciate and respect their own people, how will they respect humanity at large?"

"I knowing 14 generations of my family has made me famous in this town. But this wasn't why I or my family became the talk of the town. It was because of a man called Vishnu Bharadhwaj from the 7th generation of my family."

"The greatest of astrologers, doctor and philosopher of his times, He was the chief advisor to the then King of Banaras. He could do things unimaginable by us mere humans. He could astral travel, he could predict the future with great accuracy as compared to anyone in my 14 generations and he could read minds with utmost precision. But what made him a legend was the secret recipe of a magical medicine, which could almost bring back people from dead."

Vijay was stunned to hear this name. It was the name Mr. Raman had mentioned. He also remembered that Mr. Raman had told him that Vishnu Bharadhwaj was the spiritual master of Shankar Narayan, who was Vijay's ancestor. He wondered if Dr. Joshi knew anything about the pot or his ancestor.

Now he had more reason to get as much as information as he could.

"You seem to have great respect towards your ancestors, Doctor. It is rare to find people who respect their ancestors. People don't even know much about their family tree beyond their grandfather or at best, their great grandfather. But somehow, I am not convinced about what you say about astrology and the other things like astral travel. These concepts can only be theoretical."

"Mr. Vijay, I understand why the so-called practical people like you don't believe in ancient sciences. It is because I know these days people are using this science with an intent of making money. Hence, their predictions go haywire."

"But when practiced by people who have the depth of knowledge about this science and their intent is to help, the results are entirely different."

"I agree I cannot show you anything solid about astral travel, but I can certainly try to demonstrate that there is truth in astrology and mind reading. It is not petty tricks just to fool innocent people. Astrology isn't an art but a science based on precise mathematical and physics calculations. Astrology is concerned with the observations of the positions of certain bodies and certain points in the heavens, in relation to the earth and with the correspondences between these relative positions and the events that occur on the Earth. It also depends on the time, when the prediction is made. I can prove it in simple ways."

"Yes please Dr. Joshi, show me how astrology works, it would be interesting to see if you can talk about me without knowing anything other than what I have told you."

Though the professor noticed a slight sarcasm in the request but he sportingly took up the challenge.

The conversation was broken when Dr. Joshi said they had reached his home and he could freshen himself up, as dinner would be served soon. Vijay was waiting eagerly to resume the conversation post dinner, served by the very hospitable family of Dr. Joshi. The professor noticed it and said, "You don't let go easy do you? Come on in I am eager too."

Vijay smiled and followed Dr. Joshi into his study. It was a small room with hardly any furniture. The room looked perfectly organized for guests with couple of mats in place.

Both the men squatted on a mat each on the red oxide floor in the room, maintaining a distance from each other. Vijay was asked to write a set of numbers and tag it to a picture he drew in his pocket dairy, if he had one. While doing so Joshi looked at his watch. He also scratched something in his diary.

Noticing Joshi look at his watch Vijay asked," Am I taking much of your time?"

"Not at all, I looked at my watch as precise time helps me make accurate predictions."

A few minutes later both of them exchanged their dairies and to Vijay's intrigue, the professor's numbers and the drawings tagged to them were an exact match to that of his. Before he could look up and utter a word, Dr. Joshi spokeI know exactly what you are thinking, my friend, and it isn't completely wrong. Mind reading is also a part of Vedic astrology. Otherwise tell me how a man like me who has never studied psychology read your mind?"

Though Vijay found the number game interesting, he was not convinced. It was evident from his face, so the professor continued, "I guess you are a tough nut to crack and it looks like I need to give you more examples to prove my point to you. What if I tell you that you are not who you portray to be? There is something hidden about you, that you are trying very hard to keep it concealed."

Vijay found this increasingly amusing and wondered, does this man know about me? Is he an IB agent too, who is sent by my department to keep an eye on me? Do they suspect I did something notorious with the wealth in the vault in Trivandrum? Could this be a conspiracy by his competitors? He calmed down, pulled himself together so not to let his face show any emotions.

Dr. Joshi continued, "Don't worry it matters little to me who you are. Let me tell you something that is more important to you. But for that, you will have to choose a number between 1 and 108. Vijay uttered a number as he was asked to. Doctor Joshi nodded and began drawing what could be called an astrological chart in his diary. He did some mental calculations and counting on his fingers, closed his eyes for a minute, took a deep breath and said to an intently listening Vijay, "There are two people in your life about whom you are most concerned, one of them is dead and the other is living a life worse life than death itself."

Vijay was amazed to listen to the man speak. He wondered How does he know about things that have troubled me the most? It is the first time that we are meeting. Does this astrology thing he is harping about really work? Or is he just playing some kind of weird mind games with me?"

May be it was his ego of being a non-believer that was holding him back. But then he reminded himself to stay in the moment.

He asked himself as what have I come to Banaras?

"A student."

"What is the job of a student?"

"To listen, understand and clarify."

He told himself, "let the spy in you stay in the background. Listen, understand and clarify as a student but analyze what you have understood as a spy. You are here to get clues that could lead you to your mission, no matter what role you play to achieve it. Moreover, you now know that Joshi's ancestor was your ancestor's spiritual master. Hence, the deeper you get into this conversation the greater the possibility of you getting a clue."

Vijay then with an intense look on his face said, "I don't know how you came to know about things I have never shared with anyone. Though I still am not completely convinced with the idea of astrology but now I don't deny its reality completely. You indeed have great knowledge about what you say as predictions."

"But could you resolve uncertainties in my mind?"

"Choose another number."

Vijay once again uttered a number.

The historian looked at his watch again, drew an astrological chart and said after couple of minutes,

"Your uncertain about a death aren't you? But as per my calculations, though it was an unnatural death, it was an accident. I know you have lived a lonely life. Though you had a guardian angel looking after you, you could never get over the death of your grandfather. You, to this day, have not forgiven yourself for not being their when he needed you the most."

Vijay sadly nodded in affirmation. Dr. Joshi continued, "You also feel guilty for not being able to spend time and care for the person who has been a corner stone of your life, though you intend to. That is because you aren't the person who you pretend to be in front of me. As I mentioned earlier you have a lot hidden about you."

"Yes doctor, there is a lot hidden about me, but I have no intent to harm. I have legitimate reasons to hide my identity. When the time is right, I will tell you about myself. I do admit I am guilty of not doing enough to care for him."

Doctor Joshi noticed a tear that was sparkling at the fringe of Vijay's eyes. It seemed a mountain was about to erupt in an uncontrollable volcano after ages. But it was his training as a master spy and an Indian intelligence officer, that he could pull himself back together. In matter of minutes he was as calm as a sea. There was no sign of any turbulence in him. He was back to his impeccable best.

In the best of his minds, he decided to open the secret to Joshi. He opened the picture of the pot and the copper engraving on his phone and said, "Dr. Joshi, leave alone my past for the moment, I am here seeking the truth about this and I need your help."

Looking at the image of the pot, Dr. Joshi was amazed. He said he had no clue about the pot in the picture. But wondered how he could help Vijay, as his history knowledge didn't suffice and deemed to be of any use. He admitted the same. Then Vijay sighed long and hard, and then asked, "Sir, you said you know all about 14 generations of your ancestors and if that is true, do you know about anyone called Shankar Narayan?"

"No Vijay, I don't,"

"As per my research, doctor, Vishnu Bharadwaj had a genius of a disciple, with whom he shared the secret of the pot.

It is the pot I showed you in the picture. Shankar Narayan is the same person. I happen to be of his lineage."

"No Vijay, I haven't heard of any Shankar Narayan, but yes I have heard from my elders that Vishnu Bharadhwaj did share some secret only with one of his disciple as none of his other students including my forefathers, as per him, were capable of handling such a secret."

"He was a firm follower in the theory of 'best man for the job', like the great King Bharath of Mahabharatha."

Vijay was disappointed that though everything revolves around him in his quest, but nothing is bringing him to the next possible lead. He took Dr. Joshi's leave and was about to leave when Joshi said, "Vijay I know what you are going through, but, as a friend, I would give you some advice with no offence meant. I have seen more life than you and what I have realized after talking to you is that you are not an atheist. It is only the bitter experiences that you have had in life that has shaken your faith. For all you know faith is the power every human has with which he can turn every dream to reality."

"Only a miracle can save the life of the person you care most in the world and that miracle is faith. The same goes with your search. It is not going to be easy to find what you are looking for. But if you have unshakeable faith, you are destined to find what you are looking for."

"One more important thing you must keep in mind is you should begin your search at the bank of the Ganges as mothers are the greatest counselors. They not only offer good counsel but also resolve all our doubts. Mother Ganges is no different. She will answer all your questions."

Vijay nodded his head and left Joshi's house to go to the University hostel but couldn't spend the night there. Joshi's voice "Mother Ganges shall answer all your questions," echoed in his mind. He couldn't stay in the room—his mind and feet didn't care about the time of the night it was. He wandered to the Aasi-Ghat. It was cold, but the mind set he was in, didn't take let the chillness affect him

Sitting on the steps beside the flowing Ganges, he wondered what was he doing middle of the night at the bank of the river?"

He asked himself, "had he really started believing in Dr. Joshi's words?"

"Desperation! What does it turn a radical human brain into? I am just getting too desperate to find the next lead on my mission. Otherwise, how can I think that this river can answer my questions?"

He was blankly staring into the Ganges when the first rays of dawn broke out. He hoped that just like the sun that emerged and killed the night's darkness, a clue might emerge and kill the darkness that surrounded him and led his way. The very moment he heard a rich and deep voice, startling him out of his reverie, "You won't find the peace of your share in this flowing water. Don't stare at it. You will find your answers in that direction."

Before Vijay turned back to look at who was speaking to him, the person had walked a couple of feet away from him. He could only see a tall man walking away. He could only see a well-built man dressed in saffron. He looked like silver fox with a long silver-coloured hair flowing from head to shoulders tied in a tiny garland of rudraksh beads. Even his huge biceps were decorated with rudraksh garland. He seemed like an athlete in a sage's attire. His physique could give a complex to even the best of sportsmen.

Vijay couldn't figure out anything for a moment. Before he could analyze any further, he simply blurted out, "Which direction?"

While walking away, he replied, "Ask the Bhairava! The aghoris will lead your way to what you are looking for."

"Aghoris! Now what do they have to do that is related to this secret? What has Bhairava got to do with that pot now? The plot thickens, my dear Vijay!", he told himself, and before he could go after the aesthetic, he had vanished. Dr. Joshi was the only person whom Vijay thought of right now. Not looking at his watch he dashed to his house. By then, Dr. Joshi had finished his daily *puja* and was getting ready to leave for the University.

"Vijay! What a surprise, what brings you here at such an early hour? Looks like you haven't slept all night. Is everything alright with you?"

"Where can I find the aghoris and how could they be related to the pot? Moreover, how did the ascetic know I was looking for something?"

"Why do you ask, Vijay?"

Vijay narrated his experience at the Aasi-Ghat and requested him to explain what the ascetic had said.

"Let me first answer your second question, Vijay. I cannot tell you exactly how the aghoris are related to what you are looking for. But the ascetic you happened to meet at the Aasi-Ghat must be an enlightened man. Nothing is impossible for such sages. They would have mastered the siddhi (mastery of the yogic powers) and even supernatural powers like knowledge of past, present and future, knowing of others' minds and, maybe, much more. He might have known what is going through your mind. Believe me, my friend, he wasn't bluffing and to move ahead in your quest, anyway, it is better to believe him."

"You need to know this. Legend says, Lord Kaalbhairav is the protector of Banaras and no one can enter or leave the place without his permission. Hence, the sage has asked you to seek Bhairava's blessings."

"He mentioned of Bhairava and aghoris together to you. That means he is referring to the Kalabhairava temple, where you can find the aghoris. Such a temple is somewhere in the woods, which is now the Chandra Prabha Wildlife Sanctuary. Since aghoris, though are ascetics, don't like to be seen in public places,therefore, they do not visit the Bhairava temple in the town."

"Now coming to your first question. Why did he say that the aghoris will lead you to the secret related to the pot? That might be because aghoris are believed to have mastered tantric (mystic) powers and black magic. The pot might possess certain mystic powers. Hence the sage might have related the pot to it."

"But before you decide to go to that temple let me warn you about the aghoris."

"Warn me? Of what? I thought that the aghoris are ascetics. Why will they be harmful?"

"Yes, they are aesthetics my friend but they are both respected and feared for the unusual life they lead to attain Moksha or liberation from the cycle of birth and death. Aghoris are worshipers of Lord Bhairava, a manifestation of Lord Shiva. This sect of ascetics to be inhabitants of Banaras for over 1000 years.

The symbol of an aghori is the 'kapal' or the human skull, which every aghori is believed to take from a corpse of a holy man when he is laid to rest on the banks of the Ganges. They are initiated into the aghori way of life by a guru.

Aghoris' strange and unusual lifestyle creates fear and awe in the minds of the common men who live by the limits set by society. They eat flesh of humans not by killing but by taking from dead corpses. The flesh is consumed either in the raw form or cooked over a fire. They are known to sit over corpses to meditate all night.

There is a story of a powerful Aghori Baba who lived long time ago in this city. The chief priest of Lord Vishwanath temple was furious at the seemingly uncivilized way he was performing rituals to the idol there and he is said to have slapped and chased him away from Banaras.

Lord Shiva is believed to have appeared to the then King of Banaras in a dream and chaffed him about the humiliated and injustice meted out to his devotee. It is believed that even the priest was found dead under mysterious circumstances.

Aghoris are different from the men of the society. All of them indulge in marijuana, living among the dead with spirits and ghosts for company. Yet, their ascetic prowess cannot be underestimated. I would suggest you drop this quest because nothing can be worth your life."

"Thank you Dr. Joshi for all your inputs and suggestions. But I will not give my mission up even at the peril of my life. You just guide me how I could reach the temple?"

"I am sorry Vijay there is no landmark to this temple. I have been only to the Kalbhairava temple in the town, but never to this temple. All I know about the location of that temple is that it is somewhere beyond the Aasi-ghat in the woods. I couldn't muster the courage to go there. I have heard stories of people mysteriously going missing in that deserted jungle and never to return. No one is sure what happened to them. There are rumours that aghoris are the reason behind them getting lost."

"I believe without Bhairava's permission no one can visit him at his hidden adobe. I will visit the temple when I get the divine call."

"No problem, Doctor, I will find my way."

"Well, if you have made your mind up then I don't want to discourage you. I wish you luck and do be careful. One more thing, if you are going behind the aghoris, you will find them at night fall."

"One more thing, whenever in your life you tread on a path that is unknown to you, always have a guide, a guru or a master. A master is the only one who can lead us to our destination in the fastest and safest route. Otherwise, we are bound to hurt ourselves or lose our way. I believe the sage you met on the banks of the holy Ganges came there only to lead you in the right path. Hence, he is your guru—your spiritual master."

Vijay didn't respond except for a friendly smile and a nod of the head. He went back to the hostel to rest for a while, as he hadn't slept the previous night. Though he knew he wouldn't get any sleep, he knew he had to rest his body as he had to keep his mind fresh and alert for the night.

At twilight, Vijay looked at the clock on the wall of the room. It showed couple of minutes to 7 p.m. He picked his pistol, its silencer, a torch and a bottle of water. He reached the Aasi-Ghat, beautifully lit for the evening aarti. It seemed as if the earth was compensating for the absence of the moon in the sky that night and for the darkness and confusion in Vijay's mind. He opened the GPS application installed on his phone and tried to find the directions to the Bhairava Temple. But the weak cellular network resulted in the phone popping up an error message on the screen which read:

No connection or invalid location being traced.

Vijay had no clue in which direction to go in order to locate the Bhairava temple, and in turn, to find the aghoris. He was also sure, based on the inputs given to him by Dr. Joshi, that most people wouldn't help him in this regard.

While he was thinking of what to do, he spotted a teenager in torn rags who was smoking weed in one corner of the bank. He was swaying to the tune of bhajan being sang at the Ghat. Vijay was reminded of the hit Bollywood number 'Dum Maro Dum', where the actors were seen to be grooving under the effect of weed. Instantly it struck Vijay that he might know where he could find these ascetics, as the only thing that related common men and the aghoris was nothing but marijuana.

Vijay in his experience in various missions in the IB had learnt that the best way to lure any addict to spit the truth he or she knew was to promise them some cash to buy more weed. He knew that the fastest way to reach the temple was with a local resident. Moreover, he guessed that people addicted to marijuana or any such drug would have gone to places considered dangerous by others, at least when they are high.

Vijay walked up to him and asked, "mate, got some weed to smoke?"

He in a slur voice replied,

"No brother I am blowing away the last one I have. I am myself wondering where my next joint will come from. I can share a puff or two with you, that's about it, brother."

"Why is it so buddy? Don't you know any peddler here who can sell some weed to you? Aren't you a local resident of this place?"

"I am a local resident brother; I have lived all my life here. But now I ain't have any money to buy marijuana."

"What if I say I'll give you some cash for you to buy your weed, but you will have to do what I ask you to do. What say, mate?"

"Anything for weed. I'll do anything for more weed brother!"

The man got excited. Out of nowhere he seemed to have become alert,when he heard of someone buying him weed.

"You have to help me find aghoris, that's it."

"Aghoris! You want to know where those weird looking sadhus are found?"

"Exactly,"

"Oh ho ho! Mate, do you think I am nuts? I am not going in those forsaken woods—not even for the love of weed."

His hangover vanished in a minute and he started to sweat even in that chill.

"But, why? Don't worry brother—you need not fear. Moreover, I'll pay you enough money that would get you enough weed to last you for a week."

"Look, I am sorry. I guess I blurted out some nonsense because of my hang over. Neither I know a thing about those weird ascetics, nor about the Bhairava temple in which they wander. Whatever happens I am not going there. I suggest you too don't."

Vijay noticed that in his anxiety, the kid had mentioned the temple. If nothing else, at least it definitely meant he knew a thing or two about the location of the temple.

He rephrased his offer, "alright, you don't want to come with me to the temple, it's okay. You need not. You just lead me to some point near the temple. I'll make my way from there."

The boy was still sceptical about going with Vijay, hence was again tempted by the ace IB agent.

"Mate, trust me I won't force you to come all the way with me—you just come till the point where you feel safe and I'll give you your money."

"Alright brother, I will come with you. But trust me, I am not sure where those weird sadhus live and I cannot take you to the Bhairava temple on the other side of the river. All I will do is to take you near the temple and come back from there. The place you want me to take you is no ordinary place. It isn't only the place where you find these strange ascetics, but those woods also are the hideout of drug peddlers and other wanted burglars. It is a very dangerous place. I somehow will manage to get away but you will surely get killed there!"

"Don't bother about me mate, I'll handle myself. You just make sure you take me in the right direction."

Vijay handed the boy couple of notes worth 500 rupees and asked him to lead him. He was happy to receive the money and started the trek into the dark. Vijay handed him the torch as he had to lead the way. It took around 30 minutes to get there. The path starts just behind one of the building of the guest house behind the river. What seemed to have started like an easy walk to begin with to enter the deserted jungles, the men had almost had an hour's hike through the ditches in the woods, which were getting denser as they went in deeper.

Being a new moon day with a pitch-dark sky, the light of single torch wasn't enough. It was becoming increasingly difficult to avoid the pit falls on the way. It was as silent as it was dark, the only sound heard was of human footsteps walking on dried leaf and debris of twigs cracking and breaking. Once in a while, the cry of a dog lurking somewhere in the dark. Vijay had no fear but it scared the hell out of the high teenager.

It is believed by some that dogs cry when they sense the presence of spirits or ghosts around. It is also believed that dog's cry hints death. The boy was petrified by the dark, the ghostly silence and occasional cries of the unseen dogs. Under the influence of the fear and the marijuana he had smoked, he began hallucinating. And as a result of the confusion in his mind, he didn't notice a stone in his way. He stumbled and fell.

It took more than a couple of seconds in the dark for Vijay to realize, what had happened. The boy had broken the torch. It was then Vijay pulled out his phone and switched on the flashlight in it. Vijay saw the boy in the quicksand. As soon as the boy realized he was being sucked into the sand beneath his feet, he freaked out and started screaming as if all hell was let loose upon him.

Vijay tried talking to the kid and calming him down, to no avail. He tried to tell him he will be able to pull him out faster only if he calms down. But the boy wasn't listening to him. With no other way to shut him up Vijay pulled out his pistol and fired a shot in the air. The sonic boom of the bullet stunned the kid and the poor birds nesting in the banyan trees around. The kid stopped screaming and the birds fluttered away. Now Vijay roared, "Listen boy, I know you are scared and after falling into a ditch like you have, it's nothing but natural. But firing this bullet was not to scare you more, but just to make you listen to what I am trying to say. Trust me—you are not going to drown deeper than your waist in this quicksand if you listen to me. No one does. It is not like the how it is shown in the movies."

"Quicksand is a mixture of sand and water that looks solid, but acts like a liquid when you disturb it. You're less dense than quicksand, so you can't sink unless you're holding heavy items or you are struggling and make the quicksand liquefy more. You are neither holding anything nor will you liquefy the quicksand if you stay calm. So please stay calm and I'll pull you out."

He looked around, aimed at a strong root of one of the banyan trees and took a shot at it. He then dragged it near the ditch and threw it in for the boy to hold and pulled him out. After couple of minutes both had caught their breaths. But the boy hadn't yet recovered from the shock of falling in the ditch. He said, "Brother, thank you for saving my life. But I can't handle any of this any longer. We should get the hell out of here. Good lord, I sensed bad luck when I heard the dogs crying—I can't stay any longer in the forsaken place. Let's go!"

The boy was about to flee, when Vijay held his hand and pulled him back and said, "Mate! Why are you freaking out? You just fell in a ditch and I pulled you out. Now there is no danger to you."

"No, no, no! I did not fall, I was pushed."

"Come on, now who is here other than me to push you and you know I didn't push you."

"Not you brother, the spirit whose presence the dog sensed! I am not going to stay here for one more minute. I suggest you too don't."

"I am not going anywhere. Not until I find what I am looking for. If you want to go, you can. But not before you tell me how I go to reach the Bhairava temple."

"Dude, you are freaking me out, don't you fear for your life? Listen to me carefully brother. A couple of months ago, some foreigners who came here for a night camp never returned. Listen to me and don't make the same mistake—return with me. I am going."

The boy snatched his hand free as hard as he could and ran for his life. Vijay's patience was tested enough and he didn't bother to go behind the boy. He, grumbling to himself, said, "Coward!"

Then Vijay picked up the torch to check if he could fix it and light it again, but he saw that the bulb had broken and was beyond repair. For a few minutes he stood there thinking, with his hands on his hips and kept his pistol in his pocket. Exercising his brain a little, he recalled that the Aasi Ghat is to the south of Banaras and he also vaguely remembered the sage he met there had pointed his finger in the opposite direction he was facing.

The boy had also brought him in the direction, so he assumed he was walking to the north. He thought of confirming the same from his wrist watch, which had a compass installed. But it was only when he looked at his wrist, he realised that he had forgotten his watch in the hostel room. Pulling out his mobile phone, he tried installing the compass application, but yet again, bad network played foul.

Cursing himself for forgetting his watch and the lack of internet connectivity, he pulled out his pistol, connected the silencer because in case he had to fire, it was not a good idea to make noise. With his pistol in one hand and the mobile with the flashlight lit on the other hand and following his instinct, he continued to walk carefully in the same direction. Deathly silence had enveloped the environment and suddenly he heard a hiss!

Vijay stopped and carefully examined the ground around him with his flashlight. Within couple of seconds he noticed that if he hadn't heard the hiss and stopped, he would have stepped on huge cobra which had its hood up and was hissing aggressively. As if it is warning Vijay to stay away. He let out a sigh of relief that the snake hadn't decided to strike and end his expedition at least for that night.

He stood still and hoped the danger would pass and to his surprise, it did. The serpent, which was ready to strike lowered its hood and harmlessly passed over his floaters. Anyone who hadn't looked into death's eyes from close quarters would have had his heart in his mouth, to feel the soft skin of the cobra slither away on his feet. It was Vijay's nerves of steel that made him come through unscathed from this danger.

Not dropping his guard, he marched on in the dark. As he went ahead, the treacherousness under his feet increased as the path narrowed. To add to his troubles there was a huge boulder in the way. He almost lost his footing in order to make his way around the rock. His floaters were of no help, but he somehow held onto the boulder and gotten to the other side of it.

The complications worsened on the other side of the boulder. The pathway beyond the rock split up into two directions—one to the left, the other to the right. Vijay again was in a fix, as he didn't know which one to follow. He decided to fall back on the only thing that he believed in after his grit and confidence; his instinct. It was his instinct that had always helped him to make the decisions—even in the worst of times.

His instinct told him to go to the right, where the path continued to narrow down as compared to that on the left. It was more treacherous too. He had to walk very carefully.

After he covered some more distance, he suddenly noticed smoke in the air. Looking for the source of the smoke, he walked in the direction of the smoke. He expected some travellers or campers who would have set up that fire to spend the cold night. But what he saw there was a crematorium.

He saw places that showed evidences of fire—the smoke that Vijay saw looked like a fire indeed to keep oneself from cold. But the question was, "Who had set it up? Was it someone responsible to keep a watch of proceedings of the crematorium? In that case, where is he now? Did someone scare him away to steal the corpse, or to kill him?"

While pondering on all these things he saw a pyre that hadn't completely burnt; the wood of the funeral structure was disturbed. When he went close to the pyre, he couldn't find the body. Perplexed, he thought who will steal a dead body from its pyre?

He recalled cannibalism and wondered, "Could it be possible that these aghoris were the ones who stole the half-burnt corpse to feed on? If that is true, there hideout must be somewhere nearby." He braced himself to continue his search. After walking a little further, he heard his mobile beeping. For a moment, he thought mobile connectivity was back. But, soon he realized, it was not his message indication but the sound his phone made to indicate low battery. He looked at the mobile screen, which read:

Device battery running low. Please connect to a battery source.

Vijay felt it was better to switch the phone off, as he might need it later, if any emergency arose. Now, he would have to go ahead in complete darkness and hence had to be extra cautious. Before switching off the phone, he broke a long slender stick off from a tree branch to help himself find his way through the ditches and other obstacles in the way.

He had trekked on such tricky paths before; but each day is different and a slight negligence can cost you heavily. After some distance, there was a sudden slope, which Vijay didn't notice in the dark. He stepped on one lose pebble and slipped. As he rolled down, he crashed his head into a boulder and suffered a cut on his forehead. His wound began to bleed. Luckily, it didn't go very deep— nevertheless, it was hurting him.

He sat there for a couple of minutes tried to pull himself together. He washed his wound with the water he had and carried on in the same direction. But in his mind he wasn't sure if he was on the same path.

Before moving ahead, he checked if his mobile was ok as the last thing he wanted was to break its screen. He switched it on for a minute, confirmed it was ok before switching it off again. He needed the phone as it was the only way he could show the picture of the pot, if and when the need arose.

But after continuing his trek for few more kilometres, suddenly Vijay felt he was being followed. He was walking very cautiously and slowly and he could very clearly hear footsteps behind him. In an instant he turned around but saw no one. He once again took out his pistol, examined it, checked its cartridge and moved ahead. This time, he held the stick in his left hand and kept his right hand in the pocket holding the pistol.

After couple of minutes, he again felt he was being followed and this time when he turned back he saw a figure standing a couple of feet away from him with his palm in the horizontal position facing Vijay and as Vijay rolled his eyeballs around he noticed a few more people hidden in the bushes around.

He couldn't make out much of how they looked in the dark but somehow he felt the person standing there had a dangerous intent. By the time he could get the pistol out just to scare the people away, some kind of powder was blown at him.

In an instant, he had inhaled the fine powder and before he could comprehend what was happening to him, he fell unconscious on the ground. The effect of the powder was stronger than any modern anaesthesia used by doctors during surgical procedures, which Vijay had undergone multiple times after being seriously injured on the various defence missions he went for. Each time he went into the operation theatre, it took at least a couple of minutes for him to lose himself. But today it happened in an instant.

As the powder took its full effect, Vijay was as good as a dead body, the only difference between him and a dead body was that he was still breathing. He had no clue about his attackers or what did they intend to do to him. When he began regaining consciousness, he realized he was unable to move anything except his neck. He looked around to see that he had been tied to a huge banyan tree.

Vijay had no idea where he was or for how long he was unconscious. All he saw around was darkness. He wondered if he had been tied for days there. He felt a kind of hangover that one feels after consuming a huge quantity of alcohol. He felt its unpleasant physiological and psychological effects. His head was pounding with pain—he felt drowsiness, dry mouth, dizziness and fatigue. He was pretty sure, it was the effect of the powder he had inhaled.

His hands were pulled behind the tree and was tightly roped. The rope was clinched between the wrists to ensure he couldn't wriggle out his hands. The palms faced each other, the rope sat right below the thumb joints and the knots were well out of reach from the fingers.

Vijay tried his best to escape but the firmness with which he was tied, the size of the trunk of the tree he was tied to and the physical discomfort he was experiencing made it very difficult and almost impossible to do so.

The wind had picked up and suddenly, Vijay noticed a flame flare up some distance away. Whenever the flames of the fire flared up, he could see a small incomplete brick construction. He also could notice the glimpses of an idol in the construction, which seemed to have fierce features. It struck Vijay that his attackers could be the aghoris. He thought to himself, "Could that structure be of the Bhairava temple he came looking for?"

While he was still trying to wriggle out of his captivity, in his mind, he was thinking to somehow reach the rough construction that he could see in the brightness of the fire far away and investigate. But he could hardly move. It was one of those very few times that Vijay felt helpless. But he was not scared or insecure, as he had been in life-threatening situations many a times. He was confident he would be able to get out of this one too.

His only concern was that if his abductors came back before he frees himself he would get killed. He wouldn't be able to complete his mission and find the truth about the pot that his instinct told him would be life changing. As he was wondering how he could free himself from his captivity, he noticed a figure coming towards him. He first thought it could be one of his attackers and braced himself for the inevitable.

As the figure came closer, Vijay noticed a very fit person walking up to him. When the person came close to him, he did something that confused the captive. He didn't stop in front of him—he went behind him and what happened next further amazed Vijay.

He didn't feel any touch on his wrist tied behind the tree nor did he realize the rope wrapped to his hands being untied. But suddenly the pressure on his wrists and abdomen vanished and his hands were free. He bent to unfasten the knot that tied his legs and saw the person walk from the back of the tree to face him. Before he could untie the knot, he saw that the rope had been unwrapped without anyone touching it.

Before Vijay could comprehend what had happened, his saviour held his wrist and in a deep but low voice said, "Follow me."

Vijay wasn't at the peak of his senses as he was intoxicated by the powder he inhaled. His mind couldn't concentrate completely on anything. But he was alert enough to recognize the voice that asked him to follow him. It was same voice as that of the sage's who sent him behind the aghoris. Hence he asked, "Are you the same sage who asked me to look for the aghoris?"

"Yes. Now, keep following me, this isn't a safe place."

As the men walked at a fast pace, Vijay recalled what Dr. Joshi had told him about having a guru. He remembered how he had fallen and hurt himself on his way though he was so cautious, but now he was walking with his eyes almost shut but still felt safe. On their way, the two men passed the fire and the brick construction Vijay had seen from the tree he was tied at.

He also had a glimpse of the idol—it was of a deity he had never seen before, hence, couldn't recognize it. After walking for a quite a long while, Vijay felt the cool breeze of the wind that blew from the Ganges. He also heard the sound of the flowing river. Vijay knew he had reached safety. But still hadn't got rid of his hangover induced from the powder he had inhaled. The cut on his forehead was also hurting.

His saviour noticed his trouble and asked him to walk up to the river and wash his face. Then he would help him to get rid of his hangover. Vijay did as he was asked to—splashed the cold water of the Ganges on his face and head and came back. Vijay's saviour asked him to extend his arm and open his palm, he poured a little of water chanting some mantra from his kamandalam (an oblong water pot made of wood).

Vijay recalled his childhood when his grandfather served holy water to drink. He would often refer the water in the kamandalam as *amrit* (elixir of life). He would also tell various mythological stories depicting the importance of the sacred oblong.

Though now Vijay didn't believe in his grandfather's words, he drank the holy water from the sage's oblong as he had rescued him from danger and won his confidence. Within a few minutes of drinking the holy water, Vijay started feeling better. He couldn't realize what made the difference in him feeling better.

Was it the drinking of the holy water or the splashing of the Ganges on himself or the long brisk walk he had or it was just the powder losing its effect over time? Nonetheless, he was amazed.

Now that Vijay felt better, the first thing he wanted to do was to fold his hands in a namaste and thank the sage to have rescued him.

Vijay folded his hands and said, "From the bottom of my heart I am grateful to you for saving my life. Who are you? What is your name?"

"What is there in a name son? I am just a simple ascetic. People call me Jogi Baba. I was destined to save your life—you need not bother about it."

The sage accepted the gratitude shown to him with a nod and a friendly smile. Then he took Vijay to the nearby banyan tree where a Hanuman statue had been installed and the place was considered a temple within itself by the locals.

While he was following the sage he recalled how he had fainted. He also remembered that the last thing he was trying to do before losing consciousness was grabbing his pistol.

As the pistol was made of plastic it was weightless and he couldn't feel the weight in his pocket he wanted to make sure he hadn't lost it.

But before checking on the pistol, he felt that checking on his mobile was important as he considered his mobile worthier than his pistol at that point in time. As he inserted his hands in both his pockets, he felt both his mobile phone and his pistol intact and he sighed in relief. Involuntarily, he also checked weather his wallet was present. To his surprise, not a penny from it was missing. He wondered, "If they had no intention of robbing me, why did they attack me?"

Before he could think about it the sage began, "Now tell me son, what are you after so desperately that you didn't consider your life worthier than what you are looking for? Even after a learned man warned you all about the aghori ascetics, why did you put your life at grave risk?"

Vijay was awestruck to realize that the sage knew all about the conversation between him and Dr. Joshi. Hence, he momentarily forgot about what he was thinking.

He wondered, "How was it possible? Did Dr. Joshi tell him about their meeting? But that couldn't possible as Joshi did not know the sage. Or did he?"

A kind of doubt sprouted in Vijay's mind, "Is this any kind of a trap to set me up by Joshi? But why will the Doctor do anything against me? He seems to be a genuine person!"

With doubts in his own mind, Vijay questioned the sage, "You know so much about what I have been doing? Who I am meeting? Don't you know what I am looking for?"

"I want to know from you, so tell me son what is it?"

Vijay exhaled a long, deep breath and pulled out his mobile phone switched it on and opened the picture of the pot from the gallery folder. The sage was awed when he saw what was placed in front of him.

His mouth went dry. It was evident that he couldn't believe what he saw. For a second, he couldn't speak. Then, after calming down his jangling nerves he spoke, "I cannot believe my own eyes. Are my eyes showing me the truth? People, who know about it, believed it was lost. With it were lost its great powers. Where did you find this rarest of rare pots?"

Vijay found the reaction amusing. He found the bewilderment of the sage intriguing and he asked, "I found it in one of the treasures hidden in an ancient temple in southern India in the state of Kerala, the erstwhile Travancore kingdom. I also know that it was sent to Travancore from the King of Banaras."

"How did you find out that the pot was sent to Travancore from Banaras? And does anyone else know about it?"

Vijay then showed the sage the picture of the copper engraving in his phone and also told him no one else knows about it. The sage sighed a deep breath and said, "It is good that you didn't share the information with anyone. Not many would have been able to handle the secret of the pot."

"Does that mean you know about it? Can you tell me please?"

"If I say I don't know, that will be a lie. But the truth of the matter is that, I only know a part of the secret. Even if I reveal it to you, it will be of no use to you, son."

"Is there no way I can get to know the whole secret of the pot? Is there nothing you can do to help me?"

"Why do you seem so desperate to know about the pot? As if your life depends on it?"

"My family could be related to the truth of the pot—that is why I want to find out all about it."

The sage was perplexed and asked how could his family be related to the pot. Vijay then narrated to him how his grandfather could have known the truth. The sage seemed to have been quite moved by what Vijay had told him about his grandfather and also what Mr. Raman had told him about the pot's journey to Trivandrum. He replied kindly, "I appreciate your courage, son. But I am sorry to tell you, Banaras is not the place where your search will end. You will have to go places and struggle a lot more."

Vijay replied, "I am up for any struggle; trust me, I won't quit."

"I know. I have already tested your resolve and bravery. You certainly have nerves of steel."

"What do you mean you tested my resolve? When and how did you do that?"

"I knew everything that happened with you from the moment you entered Banaras. I also was aware of the purpose of your visit to this holy city. Hence, I wanted to test the strength of your determination. The very reason for asking you to go to the Bhairava temple of the aghoris was to do this. The aghoris are in no way related to your search."

"Then why did you send me behind these ascetics when you knew I'll not find anything useful here?"

"As I told you I wanted to test your resolve. Though the aghoris are harmless and prefer to stay away from people, they don't like anyone entering their territory. Hence, when I told you that they might lead you to what you seek, you could have found the truth in my saying only by finding them yourself and investigating. As no one from the city will lead you to them, because they fear them, I am happy that you are courageous enough to do it by yourself. You certainly deserve to know the truth. But as I said I cannot help you. Rather, I can only send you to one person in Haridwar, who could take you to my spiritual master who I am sure, can lead you to your goal. But keep one thing in mind, there is no guarantee that both of you will find him."

"He is a nomad kind of a person. He has no name, no location or nothing at all that he can call his own. No one except he himself knows where he will be. The only thing publicly known about him is his name—Bade Baba (elder sage)"

"The person to whom I will send you to is his staunch disciple. But even he can find my master, only if my master wishes to. There is hardly anything in this universe he is unaware of—he is the only person in this creation who can lead to your destination."

"Jogi Baba, would you accompany me in my journey as a guide. Your presence would help me in a lot."

"No son, I cannot as I am determined to stay in this holy place for a certain amount of time and meditate. I cannot postpone it as if I do so, the purpose of my life will not be achieved. Hence, I cannot come with you in person, but I'll be there with you in spirit. Moreover, I am living in this holy town as advised by Bade Baba himself."

"Now listen to me very carefully about what you have to do once you reach Haridwar. There is a spiritual society called Shivanand Ashram. You go there and find a man by name Ramanuj. He is a service provider there. Once you find him, tell him Jogi Baba of Banaras has sent you to him and you are looking for Bade Baba. He will do the needful."

CHAPTER 6

Vijay folded his hands again in a respectful namaste, took a leave from the sage and returned to the hostel. He packed his bag and went to the principal's office to inform him that he was leaving. Vijay thanked him for all his cooperation and took his leave. But the principal was astonished that Vijay finished his research so fast!

Then he went looking for Dr. Joshi, who was teaching a course in one of the classrooms. Vijay requested for a minute of his. As Dr. Joshi walked out, Vijay informed him about his departure from Banaras, and gave him a warm hug in appreciation of his hospitality.

Vijay took a bus from Banaras to Haridwar—a journey of 700 k.m.—which was covered in about 18 hours. On the way, he heard a group of co-passengers say that they were going to Haridwar for 'Ardha Kumbha Mela', which was happening from 14th January to 22nd April. They were going to be a part of the Ram Navami celebration on 15th April. He then recalled a day in his childhood in Trivandrum, when his grandfather was telling him about his wish to see the Kumbha Mela.

He also recalled a mythical story that his grandfather had narrated to him about why the fair is conducted?

Once, the gods and demons decided to cease their fighting and instead, work together to churn the ocean to get *amrit* (the elixir of life). They agreed, churned the ocean, and soon, the goddess carrying the pot of elixir came up from deep within the ocean.

However, as the elixir was not meant for the demons, one of the demons ran away with the pot. As he was running, drops of the *amrit* dropped at four different places. The Kumbha Mela is held at these four places.

For a moment a thought crossed Vijay's mind, "Akumbha, in Sanskrit means a pot, so could the pot I am after be related any kind of elixir."

He then shrugged the thought away by telling himself "Elixirs only exist in legends not the real world!"

How he wished to have found some a thing that could have cured his father. Thinking on these lines, he fell asleep and when he woke he had reached Haridwar. It was around noon. As Vijay had come to Haridwar for the first time, he asked a few of his co-passengers, the way to the Shivanand Ashram. He was asked to follow them as they too were headed to the ashram— but only after they took a dip in the holy Ganges. Vijay agreed.

The group walked to the 'Gua Ghat'. It is believed that a bath at this riverbank would wash away the greatest of sins. Though the river was flowing in fertile plains, the force it had was enormous, it was one of the most serene, and soothing scenes Vijay had seen in his life. It seemed so timeless.

People in thousands were flocking to the bank and suddenly there was a huge uproar in the crowd. A man was seen drowning amidst the great Ganges. The current of the river was taking him along so strongly that he was unable to swim against it. All who saw the man drowning stood on the bank, made noise and expected the person standing next to jump in the river and save the drowning man's life. But no one had the guts to take the plunge himself or herself.

Vijay dropped his luggage down and ran into the gathering and jumped as far as he could into the fast flowing river. For a minute or two, he felt overpowered by the powerful current as soon as he crossed the safety chain. But after a couple of minutes, he let the river take control to reach as close as he could to the drowning person. Once he did that he had to swim against the current. After some struggle he could reach the man who had almost lost conscious by then.

Vijay's swim back to safety now was difficult as he not only had to get himself to safety but also the weight of the man he was trying to rescue. That he had to do by swimming against a very strong current, made it even more difficult.

Finally, after a great struggle, Vijay reached the safety chain where the man's family came to his aid and brought both men on to the bank. The man who was rescued slowly gained consciousness after Vijay game him artificial respiration. People congratulated him but when Vijay looked up to find the group of people who had promised him to take him to the Shivanand Ashram, he couldn't.

He looked around for a couple of minutes and then decided to go looking for his destination on his own. He picked up his luggage and had walked a few steps, when a middle-aged man came up to him and congratulated him for saving a life. Vijay acknowledged his wishes and asked him if the man could guide him to the ashram.

The man obliged and led him to the Shivanand Ashram and left. Vijay looked around for someone who could lead him to Ramanuj. He then found a young boy there in a traditional dress. He seemed like a student of the ashram. Vijay called the kid and asked, "Do you know anyone here by name Ramanuj ji?"

"Yes there are three people I know by that name—first is a yoga instructor, the other is my friend who learns yoga with me, and the third, an elderly person who helps everyone here with their needs. Who are you looking for?"

"I guess I need to meet the person who takes care of everyone's needs here."

"You will probably find him in the backyard of the ashram. I saw him there a little while ago cleaning the place."

After thanking the kid, he went looking for Ramanuj in the backyard, where he found a middle aged man in soiled rags sweeping the place.

Vijay walked up to the man asked him, "Sir, are you Ramanuj ji and do you know Jogi Baba from Banaras?"

The man probably in his late sixties looked up, gazed at Vijay for a minute, and then answered, "Yes sir, I am Ramanuj and I very well know Jogi Baba from Banaras. He is a great ascetic. Has he sent you to see me?"

"Yes sir. He has sent me to you with a belief that if anyone can help me, it is only you."

"It is a great honour that Jogi Baba has asked me to serve you. His wish is my command. But you look as if you have come straight swimming from the holy Ganges. Is everything alright?"

Vijay narrated all about his swimming saga and was surprised to receive the kind of hospitality he did after his narration.

"Let me first get you a guest room allotted. You change into dry clothes immediately. In the meanwhile, I will get you a hot lunch. Otherwise, you will catch a cold and fall sick."

Ramanuj asked his guest to wait for a minute and he rushed to the person responsible in the ashram for allotting rooms to guests. He got a bunch of keys and asked Vijay to hand over his luggage and follow him. But Vijay insisted that he would carry his luggage by himself.

Minutes later, Vijay was settling in a well-furnished guest room and before he was done changing his clothes, there was a knock at the door.

Vijay opened the door to see Ramanuj well dressed in a neatly ironed shirt and dhoti carrying hot and refreshing lunch for him.

After he had eaten, Ramanuj very politely asked, "Now tell me sir why did the great ascetic send you to me? What is it that you want my help with?"

"I am looking for Bade Baba. Jogi Baba told me you are one of the very few people who can help me find him. I need your help."

"Yes sir. It is true that Bade Baba's mercy is on me, but no one can see him if he doesn't wish too. Jogi Baba might have told you that the great ascetic doesn't have a name, neither a home, nor anyone knows where and when we can find him."

"But as it is Jogi Baba's orders, I will take you wherever I think he can be found. But you will have to be patient if we might have to travel all over these mountains and still not find him."

"I understand Ramanuj ji. I will remain grateful to you for life. Just one request, you are elder than me both in age and experience and hence, you shouldn't call me sir. Please call me by my name, Vijay."

Ramanuj smiled but didn't commit to Vijay's request. He asked him to rest till the evening, as there was a Bhagvat Gita reading scheduled at 6 p.m.

Vijay, being who he was, wasn't very keen on sitting through the Gita reading. But he knew he had to develop interest in the so-called spirituality, if he had to earn the trust and belief of these so-called god men. Hence, he didn't argue; he nodded his head in agreement. That evening after the reading, Ramanuj walked up to the head of the ashram and asked for his permission to travel with Vijay and help him in his search, which was granted happily.

Vijay then asked Ramanuj, "From where do you think we must begin our search?"

"We shall begin from the Chandi Devi temple on the Neel Parvat, the eastern summit of the Sivalik Hills. He visits the temple sometimes; hence, we must go there first. But we will to go there before sunrise, as the temple is one of the most ancient temples of India and thousands of devotees flock to the temple every day. Bade Baba doesn't prefer being amongst crowds and will visit before the crowd starts."

"But the 4-kilometre long trek in the dark will be taxing."

"But I heard recently a cable car service has been started. Can't we use that?

"Yes that service is there. But it is not a 24 hour service."

"You don't worry about that. I'll take care of that."

That morning around 3 a.m., Vijay and Ramanuj left the ashram and reached the cable car and saw the board which said, "Open from 6 a.m.–8 p.m."

The rope way station there was deserted, as expected, and the operator's cabin was locked. To their surprise, they didn't have to break open the cabin. As usual it was left open because there was nothing that could be robbed. Vijay also noticed that in negligence, the operators at the other end of the rope had sent only one car back to the base. What was most annoying was that the car was stopped at the edge of the cliff.

Looking at Ramanuj's age and physical fitness, he was certain that the man won't be able to make it quickly to the cable car. Vijay asked Ramanuj to go and sit in the cable car and he would follow.

Looking at the system, it didn't take him much time to understand how to make the rope way work. As soon as Ramanuj confirmed he was seated the engine roared to life. But by the time Vijay could get to it the cable car had moved more a couple of feet from the cliff. Ramanuj began to freak out when he realized the cable car was getting away and Vijay hadn't yet made it yet. Then he saw the man leap and barely cling to the open door.

Ramanuj frantically wanted to bend down on his knees and hold Vijay's arm. But he hadn't seen anything like what Vijay had just done. He was terrified like never before in his life and couldn't do much as he froze with fear. Couple of minutes later, Vijay was sitting next to him. The expression on his face was as if nothing had happened and jumping off cliffs was a part of his day job. Well, it actually was.

Vijay noticed this, and to divert Ramanuj's attention from what he had just seen, Vijay asked, "Tell me Ramanuj ji, what is the significance of the Chandi Devi temple? Why does Bade Baba visit the place in particular?"

"The main deity of the temple is said to have been installed in the 8th century by Adi Shankaracharya, one of the greatest priests of Hindu religion. As Bade Baba is a great disciple of Adi Shankaracharya, he visits the temple in the remembrance of his spiritual guru."

"How did you come into contact with sages like Jogi Baba?"

"How can a man like me come into touch with such great souls? It is only because of Bholenath's mercy and Bade Baba's blessings that he considers my humble request to see him, when my mind is disturbed."

"It so happened many years ago. I felt dejected and depressed with life and the problems it posed. My distress increased ten folds when my wife left this material world,leaving me alone. My loneliness killed the desire of life in me. After some thought I decided to go on a pilgrimage—maybe surrendering to the divine and seeking the almighty's help to attain self-realization and renunciation. I began my seek of peace from the Meenakshi temple at my home town of Madurai, travelled to Rameshwaram, Kanyakumari and then reached the holy town of Banaras, to fall at the feet of Lord Vishvanath and seek his mercy. But seeking the ultimate goal of life, which is self-realization, without a guide or guru, is like wandering in a dense forest in the dark. You are certain to get lost."

"My distress increased to a level that I felt it was beyond me to endure the pain of life. My feet took me to mother Ganges, in whom I immersed myself pleading with her to rest my soul in peace. As I was waiting for the inevitable to happen in the lap of Ganges, I felt a force pull me out of the water and lay me on the bank. It was Jogi Baba."

"Once I came back to my senses, he very carefully and politely asked me, "Why did you decide to commit such a hasty thing, son? Don't you know human life is the greatest gift of the lord to creation? Being born as a human is the best way to hail and praise the Almighty, do good karma (duties), free yourself from the vicious cycle of birth and re-birth and attain moksha (salvation)? If you commit suicide in haste and disobey the law of nature, are you not wasting your greatest opportunity of attaining moksha?"

"I have no interest left in this life, then why should I endure the trauma it has presented me with?"

"I understand your distress is because death snatched your young son away who was born to you after such a long wait. Your wife too couldn't endure this pain and soon left you to wander lonely in this material world. But both of them left this world as they had become debt-free in this life. Their souls have attained salvation, but you still have to serve your time."

"I was astonished of how he had learnt about the reason for my despair without me telling him. But yet, that is not the question that came to my mind. I asked him why I should endure this pain needlessly, when I can escape the pain in an instant."

"You cannot escape the reward of your own action. It is simple math, my friend. Unless you clear your account of the good and the bad karma you have done in this world, you will have to keep coming back in different forms of life. The pain or pleasure you experience is the reward you earn by your own action. So, isn't it wise to fill your bag with as much good as you can when you have the best possible opportunity as a human?"

"Even if you think in layman terms, isn't escaping from your trouble a coward's identity? A man shouldn't run away from his troubles—rather he should face them."

"The holy man brought me away from the claws of death, but I hadn't been able to bring myself out of my distress completely. I still felt lost in my own grief. Until one day, when Jogi Baba took me to his spiritual master Bade Baba. I remember that moment vividly when I saw him for the first time."

"He was calmness personified—an epitome of peace—and an aura exuded from him. Neither was he well built like his disciple, nor was he elegantly dressed. His rags were soiled and dirty—his hair and beard were anything but well-groomed. People looking at him may presume him to be a mad man, but, in truth, he was a liberated soul."

"When I was walking up to him I was a troubled soul. I still had my doubts on what Jogi Baba had told me when he saved me from death. The moment I stepped in front him and fell at his feet, he did not place his hand on my head in blessing as I had expected. Instead he drank a huge tumbler of water and let out a loud burp."

"I did not understand the connection at that moment, but for some unknown reason the turbulence in my mind vanished like how a drop of water would vaporise if in front of the burning sun. I felt my entire burden melt into nothingness instantly and I experienced a kind of inner bliss I had never felt before. With my eyes filled with the happiness and joy that I experienced, the tears of realization and peace came down rolling my cheeks."

"That very moment he stood up and walked away. I was stunned. I wondered whether I did anything wrong?

Then Jogi Baba assured me by saying, "Don't worry, my friend! You haven't done anything to displease him. It is just that his presence might be required in some other place. That is the reason he left. Regarding all your troubles, you can forget them as the master swallowed it all with the water he drank."

"Now you go live your life in the service of the pilgrims who come to the Shivananda Ashram. Jogi Baba's words brought me bliss and since then his wishes are my command. I never go against him. Since then, I have been serving in this ashram and life has been happy and content for me."

"Did you meet Bade Baba ever after?"

"No! But Jogi Baba told me that Bade Baba will remain with me in spirit and will see me when the time is right."

"One of the reasons I came with you was because I believe it is the time when Bade Baba would see me again."

Vijay nodded! And then pointed his finger to the door of the cable car indicating they had reached the other end of the rope. Both the men got out of the cable car and walked a few hundred metres to reach a flight of steps. At the top of stairs was the temple, where the men hoped to see the legendary ascetic.

Vijay climbed the first half of the steps in no time, but then he realized Ramanuj was double his age and not even half as fit as he was. He came back and held his hand to help him get to the top. But, to their utter disappointment, the temple was empty. Ramanuj, with great devotion, folded his hands in front of the temple deity in prayer. Vijay stood beside him in silence.

Vijay so wanted to go beyond the temple and look for the saint. But Ramanuj stopped him and said, "Don't bother yourself. If he is not here in the temple you won't find him anywhere else in Haridwar. We will have to go to Rishikesh."

They came back, packed their bags, and booked a jeep with an experienced driver for their travel to Rishikesh.

While they drove through the foothills of the Himalayas, they came across a huge gathering of people. They heard people hailing a man dressed in saffron who was blessing people who were falling at his feet. The two men stopped the jeep and went closer to have a look at the proceedings. When they went near the podium, they saw a middle-aged man bringing a gold chain and giving it to a devotee.

Vijay looked at Ramanuj with raised eyebrows and an expression that asked, "Probably we shouldn't be bothering much about him, should we?"

Ramanuj nodded in affirmation and both the men got back into the jeep and drove on their way.

The roads were not great because of the unseasonal rains and it was going to take a little more than an hour's time to reach Rishikesh. Ramanuj noticed Vijay was not paying attention to the picturesque sight in front of him. He asked, "Have you been to the Himalayas before?"

Vijay nodded in the negative.

"Then why are you so serious? You don't seem to enjoy the beauty of Mother Nature in these mountains. Look around."

But Vijay told himself, "Mother Nature is beautiful but when she decides to take revenge, she decides to forget humanity. He recalled the Operation Surya Hope, when he was a part of the rescue operations to evacuate more than a lakh of pilgrims from Utharakhand in 2013. He was solely responsible for saving the lives of 50 people stuck in bus from Rishikesh to Badrinath.

It had so happened that in the heavy rains, the driver of the luxury bus lost control and swerved off the edge of the road. It was hanging over the edge and the lives of those 50 passengers in the bus was also hanging precariously between life and death." Luckily, at that point, an IAF helicopter, which was carrying army men on its way to one of the rescue sites, spotted the bus. Vijay volunteered to get down to the bus and rescue its passengers who were seesawing in mid-air.

He swiftly rappelled down the rope hanging from the chopper while it hovered in mid-air. He first came in front of the windshield of the bus and indicated to the driver to open the door. Then he indicated to his pilot to take him near the door. He also indicated the pilot to hover the chopper at the back of the bus. Then quickly getting into the bus, he first told the passengers to stop panicking.

He then told them to carefully, one by one, get to the back of the bus. After that, very skilfully, without hurting himself, he broke the emergency exit glass door in the bus. He helped the passengers as they held on to the rope hanging from the chopper. With the support of the rope, they were able to get out of the bus. When there were only two people left, including himself, he made sure both of them got on to the rope together, so that both could get to safety before the bus fell down the cliff.

CHAPTER 7

Ramanuj shook Vijay back to reality when they reached the Shivananda Ashram in Rishikesh.

He said, "Come. Get some rest, my friend. Then we shall begin our search from the Neelkanth Mahadev Temple."

To which Vijay added, "We have to religiously stick to the clock, because the roads from Rishikesh to Gowrikund are closed daily from 8 p.m. to 6 a.m."

After a couple of hours, both men set off to the temple. On the way, Ramanuj began to narrate the legend of the Neelkanth temple.

Legend has it that Lord Shiva consumed the poison that originated from the ocean at Rishikesh. Hindu mythology supports this as well. Lord Shiva knew that the poison would take his life, but even then, he drank it. His wife, Goddess Parvati stopped the poison in his throat using her divine powers. His throat turned blue and hence he is known as Neelkanth.

When they reached the temple, Ramanuj was filled with devotion. He explained to Vijay, "This temple is very sacred because it is surrounded by three divine valleys—Manikoot, Bhramhakoot and Vishnukoot—at the confluence of the two rivers Pankaja and Madhumati."

After sighting of the deity, Ramanuj began looking everywhere for Bade Baba. Vijay, like a sincere disciple, followed him everywhere. But they couldn't find the sage. Both of them sat in the temple for few minutes. While Ramanuj prayed to the

Lord, Vijay sat idle. The only thing he was thinking was of a way to find Bade Baba.

He asked Ramanuj, "Where do we go now sir?"

Ramanuj took a moment, thought for a while and then said, "I know, our search hasn't bore fruit till now and we have been groping in the dark. But trust me while I was praying moments ago, I had a vision of seeing the legendary sage at the water resource."

"Water resource?" Vijay repeated with a lot of intrigue. "Which water resource and how far is it from here?"

Ramanuj said, "That I am not sure of, but we shall visit three sacred ponds that are of great mythical significance in the Garhwali region. We shall go to Rudraprayag, Devprayag and Gowrikund. I have a gut feeling that in one of these three places, we will definitely find Bade Baba. Be prepared for a long journey."

On the road that twisted and turned like a cobra, Vijay had to keep his mind away from apprehensions of whether they would find the sage. He asked Ramanuj to tell him about the mythical significance of the Garhwal range and why it attracted so many pilgrims . Ramanuj put his thoughts together and began, "Also known as Kedar Khand, it is believed to be the abode of the Gods. It is believed that the Ramayana, Mahabharata, Vedas and Puranas were written in this place. The first script of the Vedas was written in Vayas Gufa, which is very close to the Badrinath shrine.

The Mandakini and Alaknanda rivers confluence at Rudraprayag. Sage Narada Muni is said to have prayed to Lord Shiva to teach him music at this place. Shiva appeared as Lord Rudra and taught him music. It is believed that the Narad Shila is a rock on which Narada sat on to meditate. Devaprayag in Sanskrit literally means a godly confluence. The Alaknanda and Bhagirathi rivers confluence at Devprayag. Lord Rama and King Dasaratha are said to have spent time doing penance at this place.

Vijay who was keenly listening to the old man asked, "What about Gowrikund?"

Ramanuj took a long deep breath and continued, "It is said that Gauri did a lot of penance here to win the affections of Lord Shiva. She finally won him over and they were married in close by Triyugi Narayan. This place is also famous for the legend of how Lord Ganesha came about. Hindu lore says that Gauri was having a bath and fashioned Ganesha out of soapsuds, breathed life into him and placed him as a guard to her chambers. Shiva came there and wanted to go in to see Gauri, but he was stopped by Ganesha. An infuriated Shiva then cut off his head. Gauri was inconsolable and wanted her son back. So Shiva cut off the head of a passing elephant and placed it on the body of Ganesha. That is why Ganesha's head is like an elephant's head! Ramanuj was tired and dozed off into a sound sleep. Vijay too tried to rest as the driver drove on.

In a couple of hours, they reached Rudraprayag and unsure of where to go, Vijay asked the driver to drive to Raghunath temple. It was almost 6 p.m., when the vehicle reached the nearest possible place to the temple. Vijay didn't want to wake up Ramanuj, so he walked about a furlong to reach the river bank where the evening aarti (lamp lighting) was about to begin. Hundreds had gathered to offer their evening aarti.

The sun had painted the sky orange on his way down and the lamps lit the river. Though Vijay didn't believe in divinity, the sight made him experience an inner joy that he had never felt before. By the time he walked back to the jeep, Ramanuj was awake and they went to a traveller's guesthouse. After they had settled down, Ramanuj told Vijay to have dinner and sleep soon, as they had to visit the same river bank where he witnessed the evening aarti.

Because if Bade Baba was anywhere in the town's vicinity, he would come to the river bank for sure. That would be only in the wee hours of the morning. The next morning both men were up by 3 a.m. In the next 15 minutes, they were at the river bank. They waited there till 5 a.m., when devotees began to trickle down to the river to take a dip. It was also the time when the sun peeped out from behind the mountains. The sight was mesmerizing and still was different. Most sunrises and sunsets Vijay had seen were either at the national border or in enemy territory. But now he was looking for a legendary sage, and to identify him he had to depend on a third person. He felt helpless, but the only option he had was to trust Ramanuj.

Once pilgrims started coming to the river, Ramanuj advised Vijay, "There is no point in waiting, my friend. These yogis come to places only at odd timings. We shall come again tomorrow."

The same thing happened, the next day too. So, as per Ramanuj's advice the two men continued their journey to Devprayag where their luck didn't change much. Hence, their journey continued to the third holy source of water and a hot water spring at Gowrikund.

It was almost noon when they reached the traveller's inn. It was nothing but a handful of tents. The two men decided to hire one and rest for the day. As Ramanuj was very sure that a yogi like Bade Baba wouldn't be at the pond in broad daylight.

Instinctively at around 4 a.m., he woke up and gazed at his watch, jumped to his feet and ran to the pond. As soon as he reached close to the pond, his run turned into tiptoeing and he switched on the torch in his mobile. Because he saw, that someone was about to step in to the pond, Vijay immediately hid behind a tree and watched. He realized that it was someone in saffron clothing.

From his appearance, Vijay felt the person he saw was an ascetic. He saw the person get into the deep end of the pond take a couple of dips in the water whilst uttering some mantras. A few minutes later Vijay saw something that he never thought was possible. He was stunned. The sage with no effort folded his legs, sat on the water as if he was sitting on ground and began meditating. Vijay was astonished to witness this.

The sage's body was completely above the water, as if he was floating on it. Vijay was about to get a little nearer to the pond, to have a closer look at the sage. At that very instant, he heard the sound of dry leaves being crushed. For a moment he thought it could be a wild animal stalking him. He turned in a flash to see Ramanuj coming. He indicated his companion to stay silent by keeping his finger on his lips.

Ramanuj came close to Vijay tiptoeing, curious to know what he had seen, and why he wanted absolute silence in the forest.

But for a moment he couldn't have a clear view, because of his weak eye sight and the darkness around. He whispered to Vijay, "An ascetic is meditation. What is so surprising in it? Oh! Do you suppose it could be Bade Baba?"

"He could be, but right now that is not what has surprised me. It is the way he is meditating. He is doing it sitting on water as if he is sitting on the ground."

"That is what you are amazed at? It is a power one can attain through the practice of yoga. It is called Laghima—one who masters it can become weightless and can walk or sit on water. Attaining such psychic powers requires great amounts of practice and persistence. It definitely is not easy, mere mortals like me can't even imagine such powers. The sage must really be a great one, otherwise it is impossible to achieve such things.

And you don't have to whisper, these yogis have such great concentration powers and nothing can distract them. Let me go closer and see if it is Bade Baba indeed. Even if he is not, I am sure he would give us some lead to the legend for sure with his blessings. Let us wait here till he wakes up from his meditation and then we will try to seek his blessings."

Both the men sat patiently near the pond waiting for the ascetic to rise from his meditation. The wait prolonged into a couple of hours, which made Ramanuj doze off. But Vijay was very alert and was watching the sage like a hawk. As soon he woke up Vijay alerted Ramanuj to seek the sage's advice.

The sage rose from his position and began walking on water as if he was walking on glass. Watching the sage walk on water, suddenly took Vijay to the past. But before Vijay could ponder over his memories, Ramanuj signalled him to follow.

As the sage walked up to the bank of the pond, both men walked up to him with folded hands, Ramanuj fell at his feet to seek his blessings and Vijay stood with folded hands. The ascetic placed his hand on Ramanuj's head and asked him to rise. Ramanuj stood up folding his hands in front of the sage.

Vijay was standing with folded hands, thinking about the sage's walk on water and looking at the sage in absolute awe, and he noticed a kind of aura in his face. The sage began, "Why are you amazed at seeing me walk on water, it is a very petty act. The acts including the one you witnessed now and about which people are amazed by are very materialistic. A true yogi is way above all materialistic life. The highest level of yogic achievement is self-realization, which in turn leads to liberation. I am an amateur—I still have a long way to go. What is that you sought? Why have you come here at this odd hour?"

Vijay replied, "I found something very rare and I set out on this journey to find out more about it. During the course of my journey, I got to know that a great ascetic somewhere in these mountains is only one who knows the secret."

"Who you sought lives up north and you will see him only if your determination and will are as firm as these mountains."

"Are you aware of whom I seek?"

"Yes"

With folded hands Vijay asked, "Would you tell me where to find him?"

"There is set time in the universe for everything—like the sun rises every day at a fixed time—like the earth showers herself in moonlight at a particular time. The secret you are after will also reveal itself to you when it has to. I am not the one who is supposed to tell you, the chosen one is someone else. He will reveal himself to you if the greatest yogi of all, Mahadev Bholenath, wishes so. Seek his blessings my friend."

Saying this, the sage walked away not waiting for the response from either of the two men. Vijay and Ramanuj went back to their tent, rested for some time. They gathered themselves for their travel ahead, but the sage's words:

He will reveal himself to you if the greatest yogi of all, Mahadev Bholenath, wishes so. Seek his blessings my friend!

The sage's words echoed in Vijay's head for a long time. But he had no option except going where the circumstances took him. He was a man who believed very firmly in human capabilities and his potential to realise his aspirations. He wondered, "What grave secret does the pot hold within? And how is it possible that the top secret agency of the country doesn't have a clue about it?"

Wondering if there was an answer to this question, Vijay looked at Ramanuj and asked him,

"Where do we head next?"

Ramanuj said, "Kedarnath! It is the abode of the greatest yogi of all, Bholenath, but..."

Vijay noticed the hesitancy in Ramanuj's voice and asked.

"Tell me Ramanuj ji, what is it that is troubling you? I will do everything in my capacity to resolve your problem."

"Nothing great Vijay. It is just that from this point to Kedarnath, there are only two ways to travel. One is on a horse back and the other one is on foot. Walking this rough terrain at this age for me is not a possibility, and I am too scared to ride on an animal."

"I understand your fear and apprehension Ramanuj ji, but without you I cannot complete my journey. It is only you who can lead me to Bade Baba. Without you my search will fail. I will remain grateful to you forever if you accompany me."

"Trust me sir. I will not allow anything to harm you. I will protect you even at peril to my life."

Ramanuj couldn't decline the honest request. His heart melted on hearing Vijay's earnest voice. As an insurance Vijay asked the jeep driver too to come along with them.

The three started to the destination on horseback. On the way, Vijay went back to the memory that had crossed his mind while he watched the ascetic walk on water.

He recalled his grandfather speak about mastery over yoga. Grandpa himself was a great practitioner of the mystic sciences, but always would speak of the command one of his ancestors had over yoga. He would often tell him this ancestor of theirs could stay or actually meditate under water for hours in one of the water sources in the Travancore temple.

Vijay then recalled reading about a diver named William Trubridge, who held the world record for diving to a depth of 132 metres in a single breath. He has held the world record since June 2016. It was rumoured that William could reduce his heartbeat to 32 per minute.

That was the lowest heartbeat count, a human being could survive with. According to William, this was possible only with years of yoga perfection. Vijay couldn't believe that mastery over any kind of yoga could enable a man to reduce the count of heartbeat less than 32 per minute.

He knew for a fact that only mammals like the seal can reduce their heartbeat count from 125 per minute to 10 per minute when they dive. Meditating under water needed a much greater effort than a 132 - metre dive.

It was then that Vijay noticed Ramanuj being very uncomfortable sitting on the saddle. The fear of horses was freaking him out. Despite the horse keeper repeatedly telling him not to clench with his legs as the horse would take that as a cue to move faster.

Ramanuj was too tense to relax and ease his body on the horse. Vijay realized he should distract and engross the man in some talk, as it might help him divert his attention and forget his fear of being on the horse.

He narrated his grandfather's memory to Ramanuj, who was amazed to learn, Vijay was from a family of people who could actually meditate under water. He then said, "This is perfectly possible, my friend. A few years ago a doctor from the United states of America, Dr. James, had visited our ashram in Haridwar. In one of the sessions of discussions, the topic of yogic capabilities was being discussed. Dr. James, an extreme yogic practitioner, explained a lot of things about how one can perfect the control over his or her breathing."

He'd said that making the heart rate slower lessens the need for oxygen in the blood stream. It allows more to be used by the brain than the heart. This will allow one to stay longer underwater with a reduced heart rate. He also mentioned another interesting benefit of this type of reduced breathing practice. It reduces one's appetite.

"That is why some yogis are believed to survive just on

the air they breathe. This feat of living just on air cannot be achieved just like that by making a decision one fine day.”

“It is a long process carried out in phases—combined with penance like yoga practice. First you restrict yourself to limited food and then to just fruit juices and water. Then you give up the fruit juices and only survive on water. Finally, with great amount of practice of yoga, you reach a stage where you can live on just air.”

As the men reached the higher altitudes, they found breathing difficult. Especially Ramanuj, because of the lack of fitness and his age, his breathlessness increased as they travelled higher.

If the terrain was not hard enough to slow down the horses, the path on which the horses had to walk was as wide as five feet. Ramanuj’s fear of the horses decreased the speed of the journey even more. The only assurance he had was the fencing at the edge of the path. Finally, the trio reached the destination, the sun was descending behind the gigantic mountains. A sight that can melt the hardest of hearts like butter on a hot pan!

It was as if the sun overhead that was melting into liquid gold on the snowy mountains and 11,000 plus feet down below, in the valley, the Brahmaputra roared like no lion can!

The men descended the horses to walk up to the traveller’s inn. Ramanuj had completely cramped up and struggled to reach the place. Despite the fact that the distance between the spot where they got off the horses and the inn wasn’t even more than a few 100 metres. Ramanuj couldn’t make that distance on his own. Vijay carried him in his arms. The three men decided to call it a night and rest.

Sometime late at night, when Ramanuj woke up, he noticed Vijay sitting near the window pane and staring into the night sky.

Ramanuj slowly limped up to him and shook him to reality from his world of thoughts.

"Vijay, I know the reason of your restlessness and I do understand it very well. My friend, I know that you don't believe in a supreme power that governs this universe. I have realized this by watching you during this journey. You are not a believer in the Almighty. A modern practical mind—I completely respect your thinking."

"But you know what, I am from the old school of thought and my experience over the years tells me that the saint we met at Gowrikund wasn't lying or giving us a false assurance. As the saint said the greatest of all yogis Bholenath should lead you to your goal. You are a pure soul and you have worked very hard to reach here. Hence, you shall definitely find what you seek."

Vijay nodded his head and continued to say, "Ramanuj ji, I am not restless to find only to find Bade Baba. The thing that is troubling me more is my father. His condition was very bad. I couldn't even meet him as he made me swear that I would see him only after I complete my mission. I just hope he is alright."

Ramanuj could only pat Vijay on his back for some solace and asked him to follow him. Vijay with a puzzled look followed him. He wondered, "Where is this man taking me at this odd hour? It is 3 a.m. in the morning?"

The two men just walked up to the temple premises, when they heard a voice say, "Har Har Mahadev". The voice had a kind of magnetic power and charisma to it. Both had a hunch that they finally had found their man. They looked at each other and rushed in the direction of the voice. For once, Ramanuj was following Vijay, he actually had to run behind to catch up and when he did, he saw Vijay standing in front of a platform.

Ramanuj came close to Vijay and asked while he was still huffing and puffing, "What happened?"

Vijay pointed his finger to the man sitting in a padmasana (squat) on the platform. In the dark Ramanuj couldn't see the face of the man sitting on the platform in the dark. Ramanuj stepped a step or two closer to see the face of the man. Instantly the man spoke, "Ramanuj, have you become so forgetful that you don't remember my face?"

Immediately Ramanuj recognized that it could only be Bade Baba and no one else. He fell at his feet and begged for his pardon and said, "Bade Baba, please forgive me. It was dark, due to which I couldn't recognize you. There isn't a day when I don't think of you. It is because of you I am at peace today. How can I forget you?"

The saint got to his feet, brought Ramanuj also to his feet and consoled him like a parent consoles a child. Then the saint asked, "What brings you here?"

"My friend Vijay, has come a very long way seeking for something. He met your disciple, Jogi Baba, in Banaras, who has sent Vijay to me to lead him to you. It is my good fortune that I was blessed with an opportunity to be in your presence once again."

The saint looked up at Vijay who was standing with folded hands in a namaste. He did not know what to expect from the ascetic at that moment. Though he was extremely excited to find the sage—he came looking for from thousands of miles away—he wasn't sure of his next move.

Vijay had interrogated many terrorists, successfully completed many intelligence operations, and even many a time gone into death's jaws and returned alive. But he did not know how to begin a conversation with this sage. The sage waited patiently wearing a smile on his face for Vijay to break his silence.

After a long minute of silence, Vijay finally spoke, "Oh learned one! I have heard great things about you and have come to seek your help,from a very far land. I would be grateful to you all my life if you can help me!"

The sage walked a step closer to Vijay, held his folded hands as a trusted friend would, and said,

"Tell me my friend, what is that I can help you with?"

"I am a public servant and on an assignment of recording the wealth in the temple of Anantha Padmanabha Swamy Temple, in the ancient kingdom of Travancore. While I was doing my job of documenting the details of the wealth in the sixth secret vault; I found this."

Vijay showed the picture of the pot in his mobile phone. The expression on the sage's face changed instantly. The smile turned to an intrigue,

"Where did you say you saw this?"

"Temple of Anantha Padmanabha Swamy in the ancient kingdom of Travancore—in the sixth secret vault. It was enclosed in a metal box. The lock on the box was sealed with the royal seal on it. There were many threads soaked in turmeric powder and were tied around the box. It is believed the box is protected by the gods. When I forced the box open, I found a copper engraving under the plate. It read that the pot was given to the then King of Travancore from the King of Banaras. As the man who knew the usage and the power of the pot resided in Travancore. I also found out that the person the engraving referred to was my ancestor. But I am not sure if the next generation of my family knew anything about the pot. A kind of curiosity kicked in me and took over; I wanted to know more about the pot, as by nature I am a curious person. Thus my journey to explore the pot began. I went to Banaras. There I happened to meet your disciple Jogi Baba, who guided me to Ramanuj ji in Haridwar. I eventually was led to you. I will remain in Ramanuj ji's debt all my life for bringing me to you.

I have a hunch that this pot has some amazing powers in it. It can change the face of life in this country and across the world. Hence, I request you earnestly to enlighten me with the secret the pot holds. So that it could help make the world a better place to live in."

The sage patted Vijay's shoulder, nodded and then went back to the platform where he was seated. He then again squatted back in the padmasana position, in which he would always meditate and closed his eyes. There was utter silence then for the next 10-15 minutes. The only sound that prevailed was the whistling of the cold breeze that blew across the valley.

The sage opened his eyes with the calm of the sea, to see both Ramanuj and Vijay sitting in front of him, like obedient disciples. After a moment of deep silence the ascetic spoke, "What we have here my friends, is not of this era. It is ages old. But one thing is for certain—that is, this pot has miraculous powers of healing."

Both Vijay and Ramanuj looked puzzled, "What miraculous powers are you talking about Baba? Does this pot represent a kind of legendary bowl that the epics speak of? Does it give gold five times a day?", asked Vijay.

"Yes it gives gold, but not in the way the epics speak of. When copper is heated with a particular herb that is available only in these mountains and is very elusive. The pot takes the copper to very high temperatures at which copper melts to turn to the purest form of gold."

"Does that elusive herb have a name? And why is it elusive?"

"Swarnabindu! It is elusive because it grows only in the negative temperatures of these mountains; the only way to identify it is its lustre and shine. The herb shines so brightly that it literally glitters in the dark. But it takes a very experienced eye to actually identify the herb, as many things shine in the dark in these mountains. Not many people can accurately spot the difference."

"But turning copper to gold wasn't the original purpose of the pot. The actual purpose of the pot was much greater than the materialistic one of making gold. It was to cure grave diseases and save lives."

"Cure diseases and save lives? Are you serious?"

"Yes!"

"How?"

"Beyond a very elusive cave in one of the peaks of these great mountains, a particular stone is found; the stone is soft and brittle in nature and has sand like properties. It is a granular material composed of finely divided rock and mineral particles. If broken it becomes finer than gravel but maybe because these stones stay devoid of any sun, they are softer than silt. It is so soft that it can be crushed with little effort in our fist."

"The copper, when heated with the sandy stones and elusive herbs to unimaginable temperatures form a soft mushy substance. The substance thence produced when exposed to the sun and silver at the same time, oozes a liquid at a very slow rate. The liquid thus obtained is capable of curing any grave injury or disease."

"Any injury or disease;"

The sage replied in a very calm and collected, "Yes!"

Vijay, for a moment, held himself from digging further deep, but Ramanuj could not. While Vijay was trying to analyze what the sage had just said, Ramanuj jumped the gun to ask, "Are you saying the liquid that oozes out from the mixture obtained is an elixir that the legendary epics speak of? Does this mean, being fortunate enough to drink a drop or two of this legendary liquid shall enable one to live forever?"

"No, the liquid can only cure diseases and injury; death

is the greatest of all the realities of life. That can never be overpowered by any elixir."

"The greatest of saints by the result of their knowledge created this pot."

After a long thought Vijay asked, "It is not that I don't trust what you say but could I clarify my doubts?"

"Go on my friend."

"According to my research this pot is more than a hundred years old, but you don't seem to be a year older than 60. Then how do you know so much about it?"

"I pity the current generation of this society. You easily believe what so called educated historians dressed in modern attire say—without even thinking how much truth exists in what they say. But you don't believe what an ascetic says."

"What is the benefit I get of lying to you? Will you believe me if I tell you what the sage at the Gowrikund told you? Or you want to see me too walk on water?"

Vijay was flabbergasted to listen to what the sage was saying. He wondered how this man could know what happened at the Gowrikund spring.

"Baba my intent was never to offend you when I questioned you. It is just that the prowess of the pot you spoke of isn't easy to believe. Hence my questions."

The sage smiled and said, "Strict and rigid practice of yoga enables an average human to use the immense and unknown powers of the human brain. You have no idea what an enlightened mind can achieve."

Vijay responded, "If what you are saying is true, then this will be a boon to so many suffering unbearable pain. The great saints did not create such a miracle not to be used, but to save lives. Then why wasn't it shared with the world and hidden as it was?"

After a long time, it was that the son in Vijay that was speaking.

The sage saw a kind of unrest in Vijay's eyes and patted his shoulder with the calmest of smiles Vijay has ever witnessed.

After deep thought the sage replied, "Son I understand your feelings are genuine, but who better than you will understand the shift in human intentions. You said you are a public servant. That means you are a government official. You might have seen people with various mindsets and attitudes."

"People are no more grateful, sensitive and willing to help. Humanity is overpowered by greed and selfishness. Imagine how much ill can happen if such a power fall into the wrong hands. People will try to change the law of nature in attempts to become Gods."

"Though it wouldn't be possible, they can do enough damage to destroy the entire creation. That is the reason the saints decided to hide it away from the world."

"Baba, maybe the time has come for us to reveal this spectacular yogic power to the world. I request you to take me to the cave so that we can get the herb and the stone to prepare the miracle drug you are speaking of."

"No son that isn't a good idea! The current generation neither has the maturity nor the sense of consciousness to use such great power responsibly or for a noble cause."

"Bringing such a miracle drug to light will bring grave danger to the very mankind you want to serve. You are no stranger to evil minds on this mother earth. You can very well think of how this drug could be misused by anti-social elements."

"Hence my son I shall not help you in your endeavour of bringing the herb and the stone from the mystery cave, in fact I shall advise you to give up on this ambition of yours and do yourself a huge favour by forgetting about the pot."

Vijay was flabbergasted by what he had just heard and he didn't know what to say or how to react. All the hardship that he had been trough was in vain. He again began by saying,

"Baba, trust me when I began this search, the only reason I continued the journey was because of my curiosity. But as I explored more I grew to believe that finding the secret of the pot and realizing it would be a great service to our nation and to mankind at large;"

"I had no personal agenda unless you told me about the miracle drug and its potential to cure any disease. But now even though you might consider it a selfish motive, I would do everything in my capacity to go and find that stone and herb to make that drug."

"In my view it is my duty as a son and the only opportunity I can get to repay my debt to my dying father. I was supposed to die an orphan, after all my blood relations died."

"It was only because of this man who adopted me and cared for me as his own kin, even after he had lost his own. If he hadn't have cared for me I would have been a dead orphan long back."

"I shall never forgive myself that I couldn't bring him relief for his pain and suffering even though I had the opportunity to do. This is my only opportunity."

"Baba, I beg of you to let me have this opportunity to cure my father."

It was the first time after his grandfather had died that Vijay's composure had cracked and he fell to his knees and burst into tears.

Bade Baba stepped closer to Vijay and lifted him to his feet, comforted him and said, "Vijay, I believe you when you say your intentions are genuine. You began this because of curiosity, continued it as you wanted to know if the pot would do good to the nation and mankind at large."

"I appreciate your courage, compassion and duty consciousness. You made this treacherous journey with no personal agenda of yours. There is no doubt in my mind that you are a true patriot. I also understand how much you care for your father and now with the help of the medicine from the pot, you wish to relieve him of his agony. Which I agree is not a selfish motive, but your duty as a devoted son. "

"But I regret to tell you son that this journey of yours will not bear fruit—you shall have to return bare handed. I will not take you on this meaningless expedition on the peril of your life. Moreover, I am not sure of the herb myself."

"Baba why do you say so? A man ends up becoming what he does, based on the merit on the choices he makes. It doesn't matter if I don't return alive from these mountains, but I would be satisfied that I tried my best. I have always believed that reaching one's goal doesn't depend on the destination, but on the path that is chosen to reach it. There will always be difficult choices to make, but everything in this world comes at a price. If my life is the price of my father's life, I am more than willing to pay it."

Tears began to trickle down Vijay's cheeks. For a moment, the sage was reminded of Bhishma from the Mahabharata. He stayed silent for a while and then said, "Son, it is such an unpredictable game— this life and no one knows where the play master sits. No one knows what his next move would be! We all are his pawns; we only can walk the path he leads us in."

But seeing Vijay's selfless efforts to unlock the secret of the pot and his genuine care for his father made the sage take pity on him. He felt that Vijay's efforts must be rewarded. So he made a decision peculiar to a sage. He said, "Son, I believe the greatest saint of all, Bholenath, has decided to grant your wish. He has taken mercy on you and has shown me the signs to lead you. It only could be his wish that I go on penance. I wanted to be blessed by him at his abode, hence I came here and you found me."

"Also before I start my penance, it is imperative for me to get a unique herb from the higher peaks of these great mountains. Coincidentally, the herb I am going to get from these peaks is also in the cave where the sandy stone and the herb required for the recipe of the miracle drug is present."

"I shall take you there; we shall begin our journey with the first ray of the sun. But let warn you, I can only take you to where we find the herb and the stone. But whether you succeed in bringing both of them down with you would not be my responsibility. It depends on your capability and destiny."

"I will sincerely try my best to identify it, as I too have only heard about it from my spiritual master. The rest depends on what the lord wishes for."

Vijay was stunned at what he heard; with great gratitude, he fell to the sage's feet. It was the first time he had touched anyone's feet with such great reverence. The sage asked him to getup, patted him and asked him to prepare for the journey.

Both Ramanuj and Vijay were thrilled at the developments; Vijay now had a spring in his step, he folded his hands in a humble Namaste to thank Ramanuj.

He said, "Ramanuj ji, I owe you greatly, if it was not for you we would have never been able to reach the sage. I don't know to thank you enough."

"I am only the means my friend. It was Baba's and more so Bholenath's wish that you meet Baba. I shall wish and pray you find the miracle herb and the sandy stone to make the magic drug to save your father's life."

Soon Vijay had rushed back to the sage with the only backpack he was carrying. But only after making necessary arrangements for Ramanuj to return with the driver.

As soon as Vijay was back with the sage, he was given couple of leaves that the sage took out from his rugged sack. Vijay checked his pistol once when he saw a black dog barking at him for no certain reason.

The sage then said, "You don't need it while you are with me son. Keep chewing on this leaf as it will help you to endure the cold, hunger and fatigue of the long trek we are about to begin. Remember not to swallow it."

Vijay had never seen any herbal leaf like it, the leaves were as rough as the thorns of a cacti plant and as thick as leather.

He was perplexed, and wondered,

"Which plant's leaves are these? How can these herbal leaves help me endure the hardships of the travel? I have had stints in my army days at the Siachen region—the highest military base in the world. The weather there might be similar to the place we are going to now. We officers are trained to endure such tough weather. Yet, we struggled, then how can this narration of the sage be true?"

While Vijay was still wondering, the sage asked, "If you have any question in mind, then ask."

While the question was still being framed in Vijay's mind the sage spoke, "You are looking for some proof aren't you?"

The sage continued, "While we yogis sit for penance in the caves of these mountains, our bodies need to be protected against all the nature's forces."

"This herb helps us do so. The herb I gave you to chew on is similar to the herb I said I was going to get from the mountains. The only difference between the two is that the leaves I gave you can be digested by anyone, but the leaves I am seeking for myself are not easily digestible. They require a great deal of yogic preparedness by the human body."

"Otherwise the herb shall dehydrate anyone who consumes it without the physical readiness."

As he continued to wonder, Vijay told himself "There is only one way to find out!"

He put these herbs in his mouth, the moment the juice of the herb touched his tongue; he felt rejuvenated and energetic as ever. It was strange but he could feel the change. Just as the duo were about to begin, Baba told Vijay to search for a wooden stick from one of the trees around, as it would help him trek through the tough terrain ahead.

Vijay went to a tree nearby, broke a branch from it and brought it along to support himself in the trek.

As the two went along the path isolated from habitation, the paths twisted and turned, narrowed down drastically, from being broad enough for a horse to walk to just enough for a person to walk through it. The rocky and harsh surface made the terrain much harder. It was clear that this path was far less travelled than the routes to pilgrimages, like Amarnath.

The scenic mountains seemed like the most beautiful sight. The snow was as if a pure white blanket was all around. For a moment he wondered how even beauty could be so cruel and harsh.

To make matters worse, the skies opened up within minutes, without any warning. The terrain became slippery and the floaters Vijay was wearing were of little use to him. The only support he had was the tree branch he was using as a walking stick.

That was when he noticed the ease with which the sage was walking on the harsh terrain,where he was having trouble, in spite of him being a trained officer of the armed forces. He was amazed at the speed at which the sage was walking in the rain in spite of the slippery ground.

He also noticed that he was not feeling the cold though he was thoroughly drenched in the rain in the cold weather.

As both men walked along,the sage slowed down for Vijay to catch up. As Vijay caught up the sage spoke, "There are two routes here that we can take; one is a roundabout trek through a treacherous terrain of 3 miles that shall take nearly half a day. The rain and the forest would add to our troubles. The other one is a shortcut—a bridge between two mountains built decades ago by a team of researchers and mountaineers. These people travelled to these altitudes to find the truth in the mystery of the skeleton lake of Roopkund!"

Vijay was intrigued when he heard 'skeleton lake', but before he could ask any questions the sage spoke again, "The lake lies in the lap of Trishul massif and is famous for the hundreds of human skeletons found at the edge of the lake. The area is uninhabited, and is surrounded by rock-strewn glaciers and snow-clad mountains."

"The researchers who built this bridge discovered that the skeletons found were about 1000 years old."

As the two men reached the bridge the sage warned Vijay, "This bridge has seen many monsoons and snow falls for decades. I know you have crossed many such bridges and crevasses in your career but I still advise you to watch your feet."

The rope had worn out and none of the wooden planks on the bridge seemed stable.

The moment the two men stepped on the bridge it started making a creaking noise. As Vijay reached the centre of the bridge the plank that he was standing on broke and went down 12,000 feet below into the roaring Bramhaputra. Vijay too would have gone down if he hadn't shown quick reflexes and held on to the rope of the bridge. Fortunately, the rope hung on.

Even Baba felt the jolt when Vijay lost his footing, but he didn't lose his balance as he had almost reached the other end of the bridge. The sage turned back to help Vijay up, but was signalled to stay back.

Thanks to the profession he was in, he did not panic and quickly pulled himself to safety. But he lost both of his floaters, one by chance and the other by choice. He not only lost his footwear and the wooden stick he had broken from the tree on the sage's advice, but also injured his right toe. The wooden plank on the bridge broke a piece of it made a deep cut into his toe.

To his surprise though he noticed the cut he did not feel the pain and also he found it easier to walk without the footwear than with it. The question came to the tip of his tongue, "Why am I not feeling the pain of the wound?"

But he couldn't ask it because he had been warned against it. Crossing the bridge took the two men to a higher plain and increased the difficulty of the terrain. Vijay noticed he was not suffocated in the high altitudes due to the scarcity of oxygen.

As the altitude increased, the overhead conditions changed so rapidly. It had been more 10 hours that they had trekked, but had only covered just a few kilometres. Darkness began to set as the sun started to go down at around 3p.m.

Baba increased the pace of his walk and after walking a few more metres, the sage went into a cave and told Vijay that they were going to spend the night in that cave.

Vijay agreed to call it a day and said he would get some firewood to set up the fire before it gets dark. The sage asked, "Do you feel cold?"

"No, I am surprised but probably the herb you asked me to chew is keeping me warm. I did not even feel suffocated while trekking at these high altitudes, I am not even feeling the pain of the wound in my feet."

"Then why do you think you need the fire?"

"This is a forest bed and a live fire will keep wild animals away."

"The most dangerous animal on mother earth is man, my friend and I don't think the wild can trouble us. But let me not impose on you my thoughts—do as you wish."

Vijay stepped out of the cave to fetch some wood and dry grass to start the fire but he could find none because of the rain. He collected whatever wood he could gather, but couldn't find any dry grass. He picked up couple of sharp-edged stones and a thin piece of wood.

He stripped all the wood of its outer skin with the sharp stones, hoping the inner layers of the wood would be dry enough to catch fire. Then he broke a wide piece of wood and carved roughly a half-inch deep hole in it with the stone.

Then he picked up the thin wood piece, stripped its outer skin, cut it exactly to the length of the distance between the two extreme fingers of his right hand. He then kept the wide wooden piece under his right knee and began rotating the thin wooden stick in the hole he had carved in the wood under his knee as if he was churning butter from curd.

Soon the friction generated due to the churning action, triggered smoke due to the heat generated, but it wasn't strong enough to set the timber on fire. Using which Vijay could set up a bigger fire;

The sage smiling at him handed two pieces of wood that he was using to try and generate fire and said, "Use these— this is the wood from a very unique tree from the deep end of these woods. It has a unique capability of catching fire in the dampest of conditions."

Vijay repeated the same procedure again and this time he was able to set up the fire and lighten the cave.

In the light of the fire, the curiosity in Vijay's mind also came alive. He wanted to know more about the pot and hence he asked, "Oh great sage! Could you tell me more about the pot? How was it made? How was the legendary power that you speak of instilled in it? Tell me all about it."

The sage smiled and said, "You deserve to know my friend and hence I shall tell you all I know. The pot is ages old, dating back to the period of the great Govinda Bhagavatpada, the master of the legendary saint Shankaracharya. This land and that age were blessed as yogis like Govinda Bhagavatpada and many like him stepped on this sacred land."

"This pot you come seeking knowledge about so far was the invention of those saints. A lot is not known about him though."

"He discovered an herb called Tapadadhati, the name of the herb is probably a combination of two words tapas and dadhati, which separately mean heat and being in the womb."

"This herb has a rare quality to intensify heat and hence the name."

"The saint also invented a unique alloy mesh, on which the pot in question was moulded and it was baked with the juice of the two herbs, Swarnbindu and Tapadadhati, together. This gave the pot the inert ability to amplify heat which can melt anything under the sun; not only that the herbs are the reason of healing power the pot possesses."

"The last of the three herbal raw materials required for the procedure to be fruitful is called Pitajana and is the seed of a fruit. Vyajana in Sanskrit means palm leaf and pitambar is the yellow colour."

"The seeds need to be added when gold is mixed with the sandy stone and is boiling in the molten state. It is the seed that catalyses the reaction of the final, soft, mushy substance and results in the miracle drug oozing out."

The sage continued, "The easiest way to identify this herb is its solar tracking activity; its leaves follow the sun from east to west. There is a popular misconception that the sunflower plant too does solar tracking—but this isn't entirely true."

Vijay wondered, "How was such a complex procedure was designed by one man, no matter how skilful he was? Hence he asked, "Do you mean he was the only one who was aware of this knowledge?"

"His masters must have imparted this knowledge to him, but probably he himself did not have disciples or he did not think any of them worthy of imparting such powerful knowledge to."

"That could be the reason why people like me only know portions of the process, but no one knows the end to end procedure. Probably he was influenced by the legendary characters, like King Bharath in the epics, who didn't find any of his sons worthy of becoming his heir apparent and hence made a common man his heir, though all his sons were knowledgeable."

"That was because people like the saint know the fine line of difference between knowledge and wisdom. Knowledge is really about facts and ideas that we acquire through study, research,investigation, observation, or experience. Wisdom is the ability to discern and judge which aspects of that knowledge are true, right, lasting, and applicable to life."

Vijay's brain by now had become a womb of questions he couldn't resist asking, "O great sage, you mentioned that the pot can convert copper to gold, I have been thinking of it for some time now. From what I know, a noble metal like gold was formed by nuclear fusion reactions post the big bang because of which our solar system was formed. A few hundred million years after the Big Bang, the first stars were blazing away with their nuclear fires. These nuclear fires forced lighter elements together to make slightly heavier elements, and these nuclear reactions released a huge amount of energy. These high energetic reactions produced elements like carbon, nitrogen etc. gradually. Finally, these celestial bodies began to produce even higher energy explosion in space that is known as a supernovas. Once such supernova created the first atoms of gold."

"Millions of years ago when meteorites hit earth they brought the metals that are found in the earth's crust now; Gold is one of those precious metals."

"Are you suggesting that such potent reactions can happen in that pot I saw in the temple?"

The sage replied, "Yes my friend, in the universe the sun is the greatest source of energy. All the energy releases that happen are because of the chemical reactions that take place in that huge ball of fire."

"I know what is running through your mind. You are wondering how such reactions can be carried out in a contained manner in just this simple pot?"

"The magnitude of these reactions is negligent and cannot be compared to outer space."

"Moreover, this pot isn't made of ordinary mud. It is the soil from the banks of the river Gandaki. The sediments of this basin have unusual features and the herbal mix enhances its powers. That is why it is capable of sustaining the energy generated inside it."

Vijay again asked, "But why make gold out of copper through this laborious process? Instead why not use the available gold for the medicine making process?"

"Because the already available gold wouldn't be treated. The essence of this entire process is the medicinal value that the herbs add to the whole mixture. It will ooze out the miracle drug when exposed to the sun, only if the process I defined in the pot produces the gold used. Otherwise the mixture is useless, even though the herbs are added!"

"Is the sun's significance for the process the reason why there is a sign of the sun carved on the pot?"

"Yes!"

"What about the verse written on the pot?"

"It is a verse dedicated to goddess Lakshmi, it is believed that mother Lakshmi is the goddess of wealth, the process shouldn't begin without offering prayers to her."

Suddenly, the expression on Vijay's face changed. The sage noticed the wrinkles on his forehead that were visible in light of the bright fire that was burning in the cave.

His mind took him back a couple of months to Kerala, to the hospital room where Mr. Raman the old historian told him about Shankar Narayan Namboodiri, the legendary sage and his master Vishnu Bharadwaj. His mind began racing, wondering if he shared the blood line of Shankar Narayan and did his immediate grandfather know anything about the pot and its legacy.

Bade Baba instantly read his mind and said, "Do not stress yourself unnecessarily son, it is true that you share your blood line with the great sage. You do belong to his family, but your apprehension about your immediate grandfather is needless. He was an innocent man and had no idea about the powers the pot possesses. In fact only a couple of generations after King Rama Varmain the royal family and a few after Shankar Narayan in your bloodline knew about the pot and its prowess."

"Actually I am surprised at how well the secret of the pot has been guarded by the people responsible for doing so for centuries."

Vijay was taken aback when he saw the sage answer his question even before he had asked it, but he tried his best not to show his surprise. The sage smiled at him and patted his back as if to say—relax its okay.

He was now experiencing mixed emotions; he was excited and proud that he shared the bloodline of someone whom legends consider extraordinary. He also was enthralled that he was at the verge of discovering a piece of history that could change the face of mankind.

Both men fell silent for a while—one in deep meditation and the other one was thinking what the dawn of a new day would bring. In a few hours, the day broke with the first ray of the sun.

The sage opened his eyes with the first ray of the day, he stood up offered his prayers to the sun. Meanwhile Vijay stepped out of the cave to get another branch of a tree to support himself during the rest of the trek.

The two men continued the trek for few more kilometres as the path continued to become more treacherous. But all of a sudden, the path widened itself for a furlong.

As they walked Vijay noticed a small stream of water flowing below his feet.

Suddenly Bade Baba stopped and spoke with a voice, which contained a tone of warning. He pointed to a narrow opening in a huge rock from which the stream was flowing out.

"This is our destination—this narrow passage. At the other side of it, the herbs we are looking for grow. But be very careful. Though this space seems very narrow, you will find two lanes inside. You better be extremely alert while you follow me. If you accidentally take the wrong lane, you shall never come back alive. I hope you make most use of all your senses, as you will be visually impaired because there is negligible amount or no light in this cave.

"Also remember few instructions before we enter the cave. Firstly, we will not able to walk upright in the cave, we will have crawl through or even slither on the ground. In order to avoid getting hurt by the sharp edged rocks a few feet above."

"You need to listen to the sound I make with my stick, because that is best way to gauge the direction I am moving ahead in. You too need to use your stick to check obstacles in front or over your head. I shall only call out if I suspect danger and you must freeze and stay there till I tell you again. Make sure you don't move a muscle."

"Last but the most important is not to touch anything that seems attractive to the eye, unless I ask you to. Because if you do, you may not live to tell the tale."

The two men entered the aperture one after the other, just before Baba could move ahead Vijay asked him to wait for a minute. He took his mobile out hoping the device was alive with a little battery. Also, he wanted to check out the hollow they were getting into once before they went in deep.

Fortunately, his mobile had just enough battery to let the men take a good look at the surroundings. Baba pointed to the path on his right and said it was the path they had to go in. But before they could take a step further the mobile went out of battery and it was almost pitch dark.

The sage asked Vijay to get down on his knees and follow him. Vijay noticed only then that the space he was asked to crawl into was at best as high as an AC duct, or lower than that.

Both the men began crawling on their four limbs holding their respective wooden sticks. The passage was as cold as a refrigerator as the stream of melted glacial water flew through it. Vijay wondered if it would have been freezing cold in there.

They hadn't crawled more than a few feet but it got absolutely dark, as the cave above had no cracks for the sun to peep in. The two lost the sense of time as they crawled along the passage, it seemed like ages that they were crawling. There were corners and spaces in the passage, where they literally had to creep like snakes.

The only noises that made them feel they were in a place liveable were the water stream, the sound of the sticks and their will power to go back alive to civilization.

As both of them crept ahead, the sage suddenly whispered, "Freeze".

Wondering why, Vijay did as he was asked to, moments later he noticed the hissing of a serpent. Then he felt the snake slither over his back. Luckily, it was no mood to bite and Vijay let it pass over him.

As they inched forward he noticed a single ray of sunlight enter the cave. He was intrigued how the light was coming through When he lifted his head a little he saw a tiny crack in the surface of the cave from which the sun peeped through.

He then saw something glittering in that light on the rock bed; he realized when he got closer that it was a herb and it was alive because it received enough sun from the crack above. The glitter of the plant reminded him of the description Baba had spoken off, about Swarnabindu one of the miracle herbs.

For a moment he was tempted to pluck it, but thanks to his army training, his instincts stopped him from touching it. He remembered his instructor at the IMA had cautioned him never to disobey orders and he pulled his hand back from the plant.

After some more creeping and crawling, the men sighted a dead end but that area had enough overhead space that both men could kneel. Vijay looked at the sage with a questioning look on his face.

Baba replied, "Don't worry this region is prone to landslides and earthquakes, probably this opening closed in one of those. This rock should be loose enough for two men to remove. Once we move it we will find the herbs and the sandy stone on the other side in the valley."

The sage was about to stretch his arm to begin moving the rock when Vijay stopped him. He said,

"Do not bother yourself sir, It is a shame on me if I expect you to assist me at your age in moving this boulder. I shall do it."

The sage smiled and agreed to wait while Vijay put all his might for several minutes to move the rock an inch. Finally, after a super human effort he could move the boulder enough to see half the opening. While he recovered for couple of minutes, Baba just pushed the rock with one hand the rock rolled to a side.

Vijay looked at Baba with a puzzled look, as if he was asking,

"How did you do that so easily?"

The sage replied,

"Don't look so confused. It is you who put most of the effort in moving the boulder, by mis-balancing it and as I pushed it a little it rolled over."

Vijay anyhow wasn't convinced, as he knew moving that rock took great strength.

At the other side of the opening was the one of the most beautiful valleys in the world where one of the tributaries of the river Bramhaputra flowed and at the far end was the Everest in all its glory. But Vijay was in no mood to appreciate the scenery.

He jumped out of the cave with the enthusiasm of a little boy who looks for his toys desperately. He looked around in utmost anxiety but could find nothing but fresh, green grass. The sage followed Vijay and patted his back to calm him down.

"Son, you have looked into the eyes of death many a time but I am sure the fear of death never made you this anxious. This shows the love and concern you have for your father. I completely understand your mind set. Relax my boy, the herbs we are looking for are a furlong away."

"Just be patient for a little longer and we shall get there."

By then Vijay had gathered himself and was back to his composed self. He followed Baba for a couple of hundred metres and then the sage showed him green pastures where they might find elusive herbs. But he again warned him not to touch any herb.

This time for an additional reason, he said, "According to the procedure of Ayurveda an herb of medicinal value is of great value. As it is used in the most pious actions of relieving people from their pain and saving lives."

"That is the reason these herbs mustn't be plucked as and when one pleases—there is a pious procedure that needs to be followed very meticulously. Otherwise the process of preparing the medicine won't be fruitful."

"First and foremost we need to prostrate to Mahadev. Then pray to lord Dhanvantri, who is the master of medicinal knowledge and the Ashwini gods, who are the divine doctors. Then one has to seek permission from the plant itself to pluck from it."

Vijay had to hold himself from touching or even showing the plants he thought looked similar to the plants the sage described. He felt the sage was better by himself and he by intruding in the sage's job will confuse Baba more by interfering in selecting the right herb.

For a while, Vijay followed the sage like a restless child intrigued with what the Baba was looking for, but finally gave up and sat in one place waiting to be called. Finally after quite a wait Baba pointed out the plants that were shining like green gold in the sun. For Vijay the herbs seemed like the most beautiful thing he had ever seen. It was as if they were emeralds immersed in liquid gold.

He said, "Baba, I saw this herb in the cave too, why didn't we pluck leaves from that?"

Suddenly the sage looked shell shocked, "Did you for lord's sake touch that plant? I had told you not to!"

"No sir! I did not. I remember your warning of not touching anything inside the cave."

"Good you remember that, otherwise the juice that oozes out of it when it is touched is potent enough to kill a fully grown elephant in days. The effect of the venom shows depending on the immunity level of a person, but death is certain within 48 hours."

Baba then told him that this herb he was pointing to now was the herb Swarnabindu. He then performed the formal prayers the way he had described earlier and began to only pluck the edges of those ferns and not the entire plant. He plucked as many edges of the herb as he felt were enough and gave it to Vijay to keep in his cloth bag.

Then the sage showed him the other herb Tapadadhati—it was the driest plant he had seen. It seemed as dry as a dead plant, but Baba assured Vijay that it was the right herb they needed. While the sage performed the rituals to pluck the edges of Tapadadhati and Pitajana; Vijay started looking for the sandy stone, but he couldn't find anything that seemed crushable in his palm.

Meanwhile the sage had gathered all the three herbs for the medicine and also the one he needed for his penance. The men collected the herbs they needed in their respective bags.

Vijay then asked where would they find that peculiar sand stone that they needed for the medicine.

The sage told him that they had to walk still further to a small stream in which the stone is found. As the men walked along they found this narrow stream of the clearest of water ever seen in which were these naturally arranged pebble like looking stones in perfect symmetry.

The sage pointed to them and said, "These are the sandy stones we were seeking. Pick them up and collect them in your bag along with the other herbs. But be careful as they are very delicate."

Vijay wanted to see if these stones can really be crushed in one's palm. So he picked up one and made a fist of it. To his surprise, the stone powdered in his palm. He then dipped his hand in the stream to wash and pick another stone; it was then that he noticed something that intrigued him further.

The sandy remains of the stone dissolved in the stream as if salt or sugar does in water.

Perplexed at the sight of the granular particles dissolving in water he asked, "Baba, did you see that? The stone that seems perfectly normal when in its in original form, dissolved in the same water when in granular form. Isn't that weird?"

"Of course it is. That quality of being dissolvable is what makes it so special. But why it happens is something nature holds as a secret in itself."

As Vijay finished collecting the sandy stones that he put in his bag. The men set back on their way back in the same route they had reached the valley.

After creeping and crawling with heavy bags for quite some time, they reached the other end of the cave. As both man stepped out of the crack, Vijay fell at the sage's feet and thanked him from the bottom of his feet. He added, "O great sage, how can I repay your debt? I can never repay it; it is only because of your guidance that now shall be able to cure my father."

There was euphoric joy on Vijay's face; he was on top of the world.

The sage lifted Vijay to his feet and said, "Don't thank me son, it is not you who is in debt. But it was me, according to the theory of karma, I was in your debt in my previous life and this was the way I had to repay you. Whenever one person receives help from another person, the person who renders help is repaying his debt of his previous life to the person receiving help."

"One more thing—remember not to celebrate before time. Everything meets its desired result only if the greatest yogi of all Bholenath wishes so. Come let us go from this place, this area is prone to massive landslides and earthquakes, so let's reach safety as soon as possible."

Baba just had finished uttering these words and land beneath their feet began shaking. Both Baba and Vijay realized what was happening and they dashed downhill. Rocks and boulders began sliding from every direction. Both men sprinted as fast as possible.

As they ran a huge rock came rolling towards Baba, Vijay saw the rolling rock from the corner of his eye and in order to protect the sage, he pushed him aside, and sighed in relief. But while he did so he failed to notice another boulder coming his way, by the time he did it was too late. The boulder rolled down with all the speed it could and hit Vijay.

The momentum of the rock and took him to the edge of the cliff. Blood drained out of the sage's face as he saw Vijay roll over the edge of the mountain. Unknowingly, the acetic had developed a kind of affection towards Vijay. He rushed to the edge of the cliff hoping to see his young friend hang in.

The sage sighed for a moment only after he saw Vijay had somehow managed to cling on to the root of an uprooted tree, the mountainous piece of land above him shivered. He hung by the skin of his teeth and was trying with all his might to pull himself up and get to safety.

That's when he saw an arm being stretched out to pull him up, he felt most relieved to know that Baba was alright.

Vijay grabbed the stretched arm tried to drag himself up by taking little support that was available below his feet. Only to realize that something was seriously wrong with his right knee, he couldn't push himself up the cliff.

It took all the strength in his already drained body to haul himself up. If it wasn't for his agility and the courage to fight grave situation, he would have survived and lived to tell the tale.

But the relief of a new lease of life evaporated like a dew drop in the morning sun, as he couldn't see his bag amidst all the debris nature had caused in minutes.

Forgetting the agony in his knee he went forward seeking the bag, which was at that moment the greatest treasure of his life. But all he could achieve was a bad fall on his face, hurting his forehead with a bad cut. He could not move an inch and was in excruciating pain. The sage helped him back to his feet and Vijay thought the sage too wanted to do what he wanted. He said, "Yes Baba give me a hand, let's go back into the cave. I don't see my bag anywhere; it has been destroyed surely in the havoc that we witnessed. But we won't give up right? Come on let's get the herbs once again."

But the expression on Baba's face was not something Vijay was expecting. It did not look positive. This time Vijay read the sage's mind, "You don't want to go, do you? Baba don't worry about my physical state, I have been in such situations many times. I can drag myself into and out of the valley all over again. You don't even have to worry about your safety, I'll make sure you return safely at the peril of my life. I beg of you, O great one let us go again."

The sage shook his head horizontally and said, "Son, you have trusted me all this while, trust me this one last time. This is not the right time to enter that space. We don't even know what the status of the cave is; does the opening even exist still?

Moreover, even if we get to the other end of the aperture is there a guarantee that the herbs are still alive? Given the probability that the epicentre of the earthquake was the valley?"

"The valley might be inaccessible for years together now."

Vijay was about to give a counter argument. But just as he was about to do so, he felt a shudder under his feet. The sage needed no more invitation to drag the limping man and this time there was no push back from Vijay too.

The old sage showed unbelievable strength and agility as he dragged almost the entire body weight of the injured man on him. Vijay was amazed at what he saw the ascetic do. Few hours later, the two men were back in the same cave they had spent the previous night. Fortunately, after a while the tremors subsided.

The sage made Vijay lie in that cave and went out looking for some herbs with medicinal values to set bones right, analgesic effect, an anti-depressant and an anaesthetic drug.

He ground the herbs for its juices with stones and asked Vijay drink it, who was too disappointed and sad to drink the medicine. He heart was heavy that he had lost a great opportunity to cure his father. For the first time he felt he was a failure in life.

The sage looked at Vijay with sympathy then said,

"Son, think about it, you can only go to your father only if you recover quickly. Your kneecap has broken and in this condition, you won't be in a position to look after your father for months. What if he needs you at the earliest?"

It was as if Baba was pacifying a kid crying for a broken or lost toy.

Vijay finally agreed to drink the herbal juices that the sage squeezed into his mouth and within minutes after drinking it he fell asleep. He uttered apologies all night to his father for failing in his duties.

To his surprise, in the morning, he felt absolutely no pain and his leg was as flexible as before. Both the men began their trek back to Kedarnath with the first ray of the morning; it was only then that he realized that he had lost his pistol along with the herbs, sandy stones and the bag.

This time around, the journey was silent not because the sage expected Vijay not to speak. But because Vijay was thinking about his loss.

Finally ,Vijay broke his silence. He asked, "Baba, why did I make this journey if I was destined to fail?"

The sage smiled and said, "Son, remember we do not get anything before it is time and more than what we are destined for. Don't you remember what the lord said in the Bhagvat Gita? Doesn't he say that the purpose of one's life is to only perform duties and not expect fruits?"

"Think about it this way. Every activity of life is divided in seven parts—six of them are dependent on our effort and one on divine wish. The success or failure of everything we do is the collective result of all these seven divisions. One might ask the importance of someone achieving success in all six divisions if there is no divine will. The answer to this my friend is saptamam dyva sankalpam, that means the seventh division is the divine will. Divine will isn't something that is under our control. We can control our action, but even the divine helps only those who help themselves."

"Even the seventh factor, the divine, is the differentiating factor between one's successes and failures; it won't matter if the remaining human effort isn't adequate. You did everything in your capacity to prepare the miracle drug, but nature's will was not in your favour."

"You could have given up at any point from the moment you began this expedition till now but you haven't till now. So there is no reason for you to feel guilty about it. Your father is blessed to have a son like you. "

"Baba, you can say all this to comfort me, but the question still remains, why has such a miraculous power been made inaccessible when it can save so many lives?"

"You answered your own question son, it is inaccessible because it is a miraculous power and as you have been told before, if it reaches the wrong hands it could be misused."

"Son, never forget one thing, Almighty or call the Supreme Power as nature if you please so never go wrong. All the power is never given to one. Consider this if a lion was born with the speed of a cheetah or vice versa, either of them could have become invincible."

"Being invincible is against the law of nature; the miracle drug has the potential to make one invulnerable and when that happens, man sets out on the wrong path. Moreover, the value of any great power or achievement is appreciated only when one works hard for it. Otherwise, it is never valued and often misused. That is the reason why the yogis of yesteryears kept this and many other miraculous things a secret from their disciples if they were not worthy."

"One has to make himself worthy of what he desires to achieve, persistence and the right intent are the key."

The last sentence the sage said echoed in Vijay's mind. He felt lost for a moment and when he was came back to reality, it was the same dog's bark that had seen him off to the final leg of his expedition. When he looked around he was alone—the sage had vanished. He knew there was no point in looking for him, as he knew he won't find him.

But he knew one thing for sure, that his mission of making the miracle drug had not ended, but just begun.

BLURBS

Intriguing story, conflicts and turmoil's of Vijay are very well depicted. Agree with the sage on "the purpose of one's life is to only perform duties and not expect fruits." A wonderful debut. -V. R. Ferose, Senior Vice President and Head of Globalization Services - SAP and Founder of India Inclusion Summit and Co-Author of *'Gifted'*.

The Relic, by Ashwin Karthik SN and Madhava Sharma, has a fine blend of myth and mystery, combining the best aspects of suspense and temple traditions. An absorbing read indeed. – L. Subramani, journalist and author of the memoir *'Lights Out'*.

Ashwin and Madhava are living proof of how miracles can be achieved when the mind is focussed upon determination, achievement and optimism rather than setbacks. They have written a book, this is hugely inspiring to all those who procrastinate ideas and their realisation. Both of them, to me are truly inspiring stories and I hope they realise many more dreams in the years to come. - A former journalist, Reema Moudgil is the author of Perfect Eight and the Executive Editor of the online website, Unboxed Writers.

Waiting to read more!! Curious to know more on what happens in the life of Vijay? While reading I could feel as though it was just happening right there. The story is so interesting that I was glued till the last page. This book is very different from the other books , sounds fictional yet so realistic to me! – Deesha Sangani, Motivational speaker and author of *'90 Steps towards Beginning of a Journey'* and *'She Dared to Dream Through Her Eyes.'*

ABOUT THE AUTHORS

Ashwin Karthik S. N.

Ashwin established himself as a true achiever from the very moment of his birth. He was born with a deficient supply of oxygen, which resulted in a crippling and life-long condition called cerebral palsy.

He is quadriplegic, with the severest form of cerebral palsy that affects all four limbs. But, as though to balance his misfortune, he is blessed with an indomitable spirit and the will to take up impossible challenges of leading and succeeding in a world full of people without disadvantages;

Qualified as the first engineering graduate in India as Computer Science, as specialization. Ashwin is presently working with ANZ, as a Business Analyst. Besides the precision and efficiency he shows in his work, he has also been a mascot of the company's effort for inclusiveness.

Ashwin has been felicitated with many other awards, the highest among them being the national award for being the "Best Employee" in the space of PWD's from the honourable president of India Shri Pranab Mukherjee and the Helen keller award.

Work and academics are not the only fields he shines in! An embodiment of a truly multifaceted human being, he gives form to his feelings and beliefs through poignant poetry written in different languages.

you can write to the author @ akarthik21@yahoo.com

Madhava Sharma

It is said that god doesn't give you troubles without giving you the strength to face them. It takes a lot of zeal and determination to convert one's weaknesses to strength. Madhava is a living example of the above. The man descended slowly in blindness due to the medical condition called "Macular Degeneration".

The medical condition was only potent enough to snatch away the man's sight but not his vision or his love towards life or the dignity with which he chose to lead it. After successfully qualifying as a commerce graduate, Madhava has walked various paths of life in order to respectfully earn a livelihood.

He has worked in various organizations at various positions, he has successfully worked as an insurance agent and has a LIC agent profile for over two decades. He has also been a successful business man for some time.

Currently he holds the position of a senior officer in the admin department of a MNC called Mphasis.

Madhava is an inspiring personality, he believes in returning what he has received from the society and hence is serving at various social organizations and NGO's that work towards the betterment of the specially abled.

His poetry in Kannada not only entertains and inspires one and all. But also conveys a very strong and positive message to the society.

 you can write to the author @ madhavarao.a@gmail.com

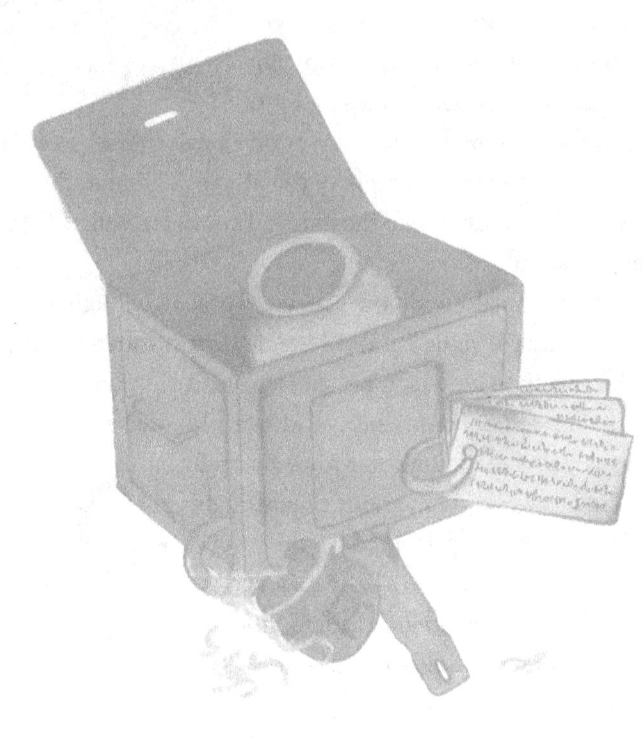

the RELIC

...the eternal search

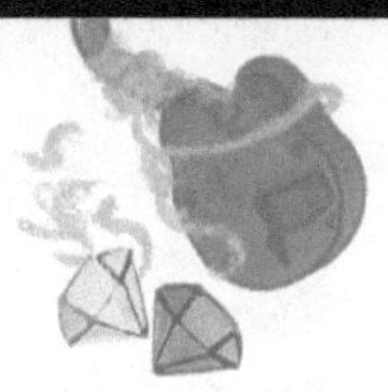

Ashwin Karthik

&

Madhava Sharma

Did you like the book

Email your
questions, experiences, and suggestions
to the author at
akarthik21@yahoo.com
madhavarao.a@gmail.com

CROWD-FUNDERS

(NAMES LISTED ALPHABETICALLY)

- Abhijith M L Gowda
- Abhishek Bapu
- Abhishek J
- Adithi Darshan
- Aishwarya Iyer
- Ajay Varijam
- Akhilesh Nayak
- Alistair Collaco
- Anirudd Naragund
- Anirudh Purohit
- Apratim Roy Chowdhury
- Aquib Pasha
- Aravind Dixit
- Arumugam
  Subramanyam
- Arun H
- Arun S P
- Aruna S
- Arvindraj A R
- Arya Kundu
- Ashwin Kumar Bonup
- Ashwin Mohan
- Ashwin S
- Ashwini Ganeshan
- Asmita Karanje
- Bharath Sharma
- Bharathi Prathap
- Bharathi Sridhar
- Bhavya Venkatesh
- Biju George

- Chandra Shekhar
- Chetan H M
- Chethan C T
- Chethan Kumar
- Daniel Mathew
- Deepak Balain
- Deepak Kumar
- Devang Adak
- Dilip Raj
- Disha Sangani
- Divya Savanth
- Divya G
- Dr. Vinayaka N S
- Dwarakanath Hassan
  Srinivas Murthy
- Flora George
- Ganesh Kamath
- Gayathri A M
- Geetha Raju
- Geo Paul
- George Sebastian
- Gerad Vinod Kumar
- Girish Kumar S
- Guru Prasad
- Guruprasad Hosurkar
- Gururaj Killi
- Gururaj Rao
- Habeeba Pasha
- Hariprasad Gajapathy
- Harish Channabasappa

- Harish Lakshmaiah
- Harsha B R
- Hema Veerakariyappa
- Hema K V
- Hema Vaman
- Hemanth
  Aswathanarayana
- Jagdeep N
- Jatin Aluvalia
- Kalesh Kumar S G
- Kanchan Pradeep
- Kantharaj L N
- Karthik Parameswaran
- Kartik Bhargav
- Kavitha Ramesh
- Keerthi Kumar S
- Khushmita Sanghvi
- Kiran V
- Kiran Ghatage
- Kumar G Rao
- Kumaraswamy A
- Lakshmi Balaji
- Lakshmi Krishna Mohan
  Ponnapalli
- Lakshmi Murthy
- Lakshmi Yallampalli
- Leos Varghese
- Lokesh M
- Madhura Chatrapathy
- Madhura Mohan

- Madhura Prasad
- Mahesha M
- Mallegowda Sunil Kumar
- Mallikarjuna C
- Mamatha Santosh
- Manish B M
- Manishkumar Prajapati
- Manoj Venkatraman
- Minakshi Jain
- Mohan Rao
- Muralidhar C S
- Nagaraja K R
- Nakul Shinde
- Namitha Mahesh
- Narayanan Iyengar
- Neha Rustagi
- Nikul Patel
- Nishant Rastogi
- P Sheela
- Palak Maheria
- Paul Vinod
- Pooja Kiran
- Prabha Verghese
- Prabha Nagaraj
- Praneeth Shetty
- Prasanna Kumar
- Prashanth Chowdappa
- Praveen Menon
- Preethi Shetty
- Preksha Rajendra
- Priyadarshini Kiran Magavi
- Punith C M Gowda
- Radhika Sanàth
- Raghavendra Joshi
- Raghavendra Machani
- Ragothaman Ramachandran
- Rajalakshmi Badrinath
- Rajani K B
- Rajeev Iyer
- Rajeshkumar Pilla
- Rakesh Singh
- Rakshita D'souza
- Ram Kishan Singh
- Ramachandra H R
- Ramesh Aravind
- Ramesh Antoo
- Ramesh Srinivasan
- Ramya Ajay
- Ravi Monteiro
- Ravikumar B
- Rekha M
- Rekha Shashidhar Hiremath
- Sachin Tendulkar
- Sagar Dudhedia
- Sahana K N
- Sameer Mandviya
- Sandesha B G
- Sandra Edwards
- Sangeetha Hanchate
- Sanjay Dora
- Sanjay Purandare
- Santhosh Goruntlu
- Santhosh Kumar
- Sapna Rao
- Sartaj Sekhon
- Sarvesh Tv
- Savitha Venkatesh
- Seetha Lakshmi
- Shadakshari B N
- Shagun Ganapathy
- Shailaja Pai
- Shankar S N
- Shantha N
- Shashi Harsha
- Shashi Kiran
- Shilpa Krishnaswamy
- Shiva Prasad
- Shrikant Kini
- Shubhakara V
- Shwetha Gopi Bn
- Shwetha Rosario
- Simon Shailendra
- Siri Manjunath
- Skanda Rao
- Smijesh U
- Smitha H S
- Somashekar N T

- Sree Lakshmi M
- Sridhar Sundaram
- Srihariharan Prasath
- Srikanth Manjunath
- Srikar K S
- Srilatha Raamaprasad
- Suchetha U J
- Sudeep R
- Sujatha Ravindra
- Suma Sudeep
- Sumanlatha Sanghi
- Sumanth K
- Sunil Prabhakaran
- Supreet Agera
- Suresh Muniraj
- Sushma A V
- Swaminathan Subramaniam
- Swapnil Diwate
- Swarjeet Salagode
- Swathi N R
- Uma Bhaktha
- Uma Raghavendran
- Varghese Kuruvila
- Varsha Tiwari
- Veena Muddapur
- Venkatesh S K
- Venu Nath M L
- Vibha Balasubbaraman
- Vijay N Manjunath
- Viji Varghese
- Vikas Padale
- Vikram Sharma
- Vinay Kumar
- Vinay Simha
- Vinayachandra Menon
- Vinayak Bhat
- Vinod Anthony
- Yogesh Karbhari

www.ingramcontent.com/pod-product-compliance
Lightning Source LLC
LaVergne TN
LVHW090406160726
843469LV00038B/539